CHARLIE CRUMP
CODEBREAKER!

J D R Swift

First published in 2015

ISBN: 1512089281
ISBN-13: 978-1512089288

SECRET HIDDEN MESSAGE

CAN YOU FIND IT?

One of the characters in this book has passed on a further hidden message. Decode it and tell me what it says to receive your own personalised codebreaking diploma!

(Hint: "I ventured to tell everyone")

JDRSWIFT@GMAIL.COM

To Amber, Dewi, Ffion, Greg, Hamilton, Iris, Jacob, Joe,
Rhys, Robin, Sam & Tom

Guardians of the Future

1

Sometimes, even in the middle of the darkest and windiest winter night, Drakepuddle Farm seemed to stand out like a beacon on the side of a hill. Once in a while, the moonlight would shine so brightly off the whitewashed walls, it was as if a silvery-white fire was burning uncontrollably on the hillside, crackling and flickering behind a thorny screen of rustling branches. Every now and again, it shone so brightly that it looked like the moon itself might be trying to hide behind the waving arms of the trees and bushes.

It wasn't like that today though. The branches were calm, and lush, green leaves hung from them like a thick camouflage. Even so, the way the bright July sun reflected off the gleaming walls through the gaps in the hedges and trees, made the farm stand out like a huge mirror, glinting on the hillside. Sometimes you could see it for miles around, which wasn't really how it should be at all.

Drakepuddle Farm wasn't the type of building that ought to be drawing attention to itself.

Not considering what it concealed and who lived there.

Of course, none of this mattered to Charlie Crump. All he knew was that Drakepuddle Farm was his uncle's home and that his uncle was a very clever man. He'd rebuilt Charlie's bike one afternoon, using spare car parts, a few old computer circuits he had lying around and some clever gadgetry.

Charlie leant his bike against the door and unclipped the computer. The lights flashed and the bell pinged twice, not that anyone would have even the slightest chance of stealing it from Drakepuddle.

He smiled as he read the misspelled sign above the door where his bike was locked.

His uncle was indeed a very clever man.

A very clever man who had never been to a proper school.

Charlie Crump – Codebreaker!

2

Charlie tucked the bike controller in his pocket and ran around the side of the farmhouse and in through the back door.

Someone was talking in the kitchen and, although it didn't sound like an argument, the voices were definitely raised, and they sounded very serious.

'But look! It's addressed to you.' Charlie recognized his uncle talking.

'I know, but there might be more than one—'

Uncle and the other man stopped talking.

'We didn't hear you come in, Charlie. Godfrey and I were just talking about ...'

'Holidays,' the other man interrupted. He snapped his head around to face Charlie. 'I was just showing this postcard to your uncle. It's from an old ... er ... work colleague of ours.' The man's expression changed suddenly, as if he'd just been nudged in the ribs by someone, to remind him to smile.

Godfrey Blessings was a friend of Charlie's uncle and one of the slightly odd characters who lived in the nearby village of Great Disbury. As usual, he was dressed strangely: he looked like he'd never got the hang of choosing clothes that matched or even fitted properly. Charlie silently read the big, bold words on the front of the baggy t-shirt. They were printed underneath a colourful picture of a trophy:

Allsford and District Annual Quiz Team Challenge

GDGs	*12*
LDLs	*Nil*

Underneath the picture, in much smaller letters, there was more writing. Charlie had to squint to read what it said:

Great Disbury Guardians: Reigning champions!
Little Disbury Losers: Should have tried harder at school!

He was wearing gloves too, but it was the middle of summer. And those flashy boots! Who did he think he was? They were the type of boots racing drivers wore; only these were bright gold in colour. *Racing driver's boots on a man in his* … Charlie didn't know how old Godfrey Blessings was, but one thing was for sure: he was way too old to be driving racing cars.

Godfrey Blessings stared back at Charlie for a few moments. Charlie shuffled, wondering if he should say something.

Uncle spoke first. 'We'll be finished in a minute. Your auntie's been busy … bakin'. Why don't you go and see if she's set up the table in the garden.'

'Great! Cakes!' Charlie said, turning towards one of the many doors leading out of the kitchen. *Yeah, right!* He knew where a nosey twelve-year-old wasn't welcome.

As soon as they thought he was out of earshot, the two men continued their conversation,

'This could be serious; very serious. A breach of this kind could put everything at risk. It could put *everyone* at risk!' Godfrey Blessings said.

'But who could have broken in? The security is state of the art.'

'Minatauri. Who else? There's no one else still around who would know how the security worked.'

Charlie hovered by the back door, behind a large wooden dresser, from where he could hear everything.

'What about Flack? He knew how the security worked. And why didn't they take anything?'

'Flack's dead. You know that. And maybe whoever it was didn't find what they were looking for. All of the dangerous stuff is ... you know ... safe anyway.'

'Maybe the security guard triggered the system himself.'

'Unlikely! They go through the CCTV and security records with a fine toothpick. If there's anything unusual they're bound to pick it up.'

Everyone could be put at risk? Charlie thought. *Who was everyone?'*

'Why did the curator send the postcard to you though?' Charlie heard Uncle say.

'It could just be a coincidence. At least they didn't get away with anything.'

'Leave it with me. I'll have another look at it. Where's Tango when you need her? She'd know if there's anything else he's trying to tell us.'

Charlie heard the two voices become muffled as they

walked from the kitchen towards one of the doors: the one Uncle always called the 'front door'. The real front door hadn't been used for years of course. If they had managed to open it, the two men would have knocked Charlie's bike over, as it was safely locked up, underneath the misspelled sign.

Charlie crept back into the centre of the kitchen. He could still hear the faint voices of the two men.

It was still there on the table.

It's only a postcard, he thought.

As he stared at the card, the kitchen window slammed shut. The card wobbled slightly in the breeze and slid a couple of inches along the table, towards him.

It was as if, somehow, it wanted him to read it.

He took a step closer.

What could put everyone at risk?

He looked around the room. He was definitely alone.

Surely there was nothing wrong with reading a postcard. It wasn't like it was a letter. It wasn't even in an envelope!

There was a picture on the front; an aerial photograph of something that looked like a beach. Charlie didn't recognize it. It looked like there was something wrong with the printing too. The colours didn't quite line up properly and there was a strange tint, as if the postcard had been left out in the sun for too long, on a rack outside a tourist souvenir shop.

He read the caption underneath the grainy photograph:

Flying Fish Cove, Capital of Christmas Island.

He flipped the card over and read the address:

Archives Department
Ministry of Defence
Whitehall
LONDON
SW1A 2HB
GB

Wondering why his uncle or Godfrey Blessings had a postcard addressed to the Ministry of Defence, Charlie read on:

Blimey, it's hot! initially too hot!
Reckon it's over 100 degrees.
Everyone very friendly. Always cheerful!
Can't wait until tomorrow!
Having a go at scuba diving!
henry

The writing was neat; *very* neat. It looked like whoever had written this card certainly didn't share the same rushed, scruffy handwriting that Charlie's teachers were always complaining about.

There was something about it though … the way it was written.

He read the card again.

It *was* strange. Somewhere in his mind, something was stirring. As if a part of his brain was waking from a long, deep sleep.

'Charlie! What are you doing?'

He hadn't heard his uncle come back into the room.

Charlie dropped the postcard and took a couple of swipes at it, to try and stop it fluttering to the floor. 'I just wanted to have a look at the postcard.' He bent down to pick it up.

Uncle didn't say anything. Instead, he just stood there, staring, like someone who had just got in and stumbled across a burglar filling a sack with the family jewellery.

'I'm sorry. I just wanted to see the picture, where it was from.' Charlie knew he hadn't sounded at all convincing.

Uncle's glasses didn't conceal the disapproval in his eyes. He twiddled a pencil perched above his ear, attached to the spectacles by a clip. Charlie knew he was going to have to explain himself.

'Shouldn't it say UK?' he blurted the words out the instant they came into his mind.

'Hmmm,' Uncle said. 'What exactly do you mean?'

Weird! He'd expected his uncle to be angry but, instead, he sounded calm, unruffled, almost … *encouraging*.

'I mean shouldn't it say UK? You know … for *United Kingdom* … instead of GB.'

'*Precisely!*' Charlie's uncle yanked the pencil from the clip and tapped it against the rim of his glasses. 'Whoever sent this postcard knew the full address of the Archives Department at the Ministry of Defence. Then they wrote 'GB' instead of 'UK'. Not only that, they highlighted their mistake by writing it in big bold letters and then underlinin' it. That were no mistake: the sender wanted to write GB, and he wanted someone to notice!'

How logically and quickly his uncle's mind seemed to

work: very different to his own slow and muddled thoughts. 'So why did he write it then?' Charlie asked.

'Why else would he write it? He did it because it *is* part of the address, of course!'

If anything had stirred in Charlie's mind before, it decided to roll over and go back to sleep. 'What do you mean it *is* part of the address? I thought you said ...'

'You're assuming GB is a country.' Uncle paused, slowly taking the postcard from Charlie's hand. 'It ain't. *GB* is the intended recipient — a person — and about three minutes ago I was talking to him, *in this very room!*'

'GB is Godfrey Blessings?' Charlie asked.

'Did you notice anything else about that postcard that seemed at all ... *odd?*' Uncle said, seeming to ignore the question.

'No, not really.' But what was this thing that could put everything at risk? And what could put *everyone* at risk?

'Excellent! Come on. Your auntie knew you were comin'. There's bound to be summat more interestin' than reading other people's post goin' on in the garden!'

3

Charlie smelt the freshly baked cakes long before he saw his auntie carrying the tray towards the garden table. How did she always manage to look so smart? Surely, around town, people must always have thought she was off to some kind of posh lunch, maybe even a wedding. No one would guess she was really going to the hardware shop, to pick up some welding gauntlets or some axle grease for one of the Drakepuddle tractors.

'Eccles cakes!' Uncle said, rubbing his hands together. 'My favourite, *flaky flies' graveyards.*'

Auntie placed the cake tray on the table, gently nudging aside one of her cats, which had been dozing on the chair.

'Have one quick, before your uncle eats them all,' she said.

'Summat special about still-warm cakes, eh!' Uncle said. 'You know … like they'd rather be eaten than go cold.'

Charlie helped himself to a cake from the tray.

'Who are the Mina—?' he started to ask.

'So how's school?' Auntie interrupted, unfolding a napkin and placing it over her knee.

'Er, yeah, okay, I suppose. Well, apart from Maths, of course.' Charlie noticed that Uncle had stopped eating and was tapping his fingers on the table. 'I can't wait for the summer holidays. Rhodri's really looking forward to it too.'

'Great! Is Poppy bringing a friend?' Auntie asked. 'It wouldn't be fair if you brought a friend along but Poppy didn't.'

'I'm not sure. She said she might bring Bryony.' Auntie was right. Not only wouldn't it be fair, it wouldn't be bearable either. 'Oh, and Rhodri was asking what we're going to be doing,' Charlie said.

Charlie's aunt flicked a quick sideways glance at

Uncle. 'Well, we were thinking that we might take the Number Ten to—'

'What's wrong with Maths? It ain't still Snottyborne, is it?' Uncle interrupted. 'She tried to get onto the team a while ago. Told her to take a hike! Only thing she knew anythin' about at all was Maths, and she didn't know a whole lot about that either, according to Tilly. Think she joined the Little Disbury lot in the end.'

'*Snitterborne!*' Charlie corrected. 'She's asked me to learn some stupid number by Monday morning, just because of what Allsop said last week. It was nothing to do with me.'

'What number?' Uncle asked.

'Something to do with circles.'

'Oh, you're still talkin' about circles are you? Probably talkin' about pi. I know a poem that'll help you learn that,' said Uncle. He licked his finger and started stabbing the crumbs on his plate with it. 'Pie. I wish *I* could determine pi. *Eureka!* cried the great inventor. Christmas pudding, Christmas pie!'

'*What?*' Charlie said.

'Three point one four one five nine two six five three five eight nine seven nine three. It's easy as anythin' if you remember the poem. Just count the letters of each word. Pie, three; I, one; wish, four; I one again. Just remember there's no *E* in the second pie!'

'That's it! Can you write it down for me?' Charlie asked. 'So I can learn it for Snitters.'

'I'll swap it for that last cake!' And before waiting for a response, Uncle snatched the last cake from the tray.

The two sat listening to Auntie talking for a while

about Mavis Muttersby, the class bully in her own school when she had been a girl.

'Very nasty young lady; used to flush our sandwiches down the loo. I remember one time a few of us decided to …'

Charlie's thoughts had started wandering. As he stared at the ducks, which were sunbathing by the side of the pond, another thought suddenly came into his mind. Before he knew it, the words were already out:

'Who's Flack?' It had been more like a sneeze than a question, but he could tell by the expression on his uncle and aunt's faces that he'd said something wrong. They'd put their cups down on their saucers and were looking at him as if he really had sneezed all over them, or worse. He doubted they'd have looked any more shocked if he'd just been sick on his auntie's fancy, lace tablecloth.

'Who? What are you on about, Charlie?' Auntie replied eventually.

'Flack and the Minatauri. I heard you talking about them, Uncle, to Mr Blessings. You said the break-in had all the hallmarks of a Minatauri operation.'

'Just a bunch of old troublemakers, Charlie. Nothing for you to be worryin' about. Eavesdroppin' on our little chat as well as readin' our post, were you?' He stood up to leave the table and turned to Auntie. 'That reminds me. I saw a couple of rats by the Red Barn earlier. Don't want 'em fiddlin' with what's in there, chewin' through the wires and scratchin' the paint. The chickens wouldn't be very happy about that!'

'Not again! I'll deal with them later. Perhaps Charlie can put some bait down when he collects the eggs,'

Auntie replied.

When Charlie and his auntie eventually got up, they walked silently into the kitchen. Charlie was about to dash up the stairs to his uncle's Ideas Room, when Auntie turned to him.

'Sit down for a minute,' she said. 'It's best you don't mention the Minatauri and never say the name *Flack* in front of your uncle.'

'Why?' Charlie asked.

'One day, Charlie, he might tell you, but unless he brings it up, never mention it again. In the meantime, tell me about Maths and Mrs Snitterborne.'

4

Auntie got up from the kitchen table after listening to everything Charlie had said about his awful lesson the previous week.

'Oh, what a gruesome woman. She sounds like a right bully.'

'She's just got it in for me for some reason: her and Allsop.'

'You mentiond him before. He's a nasty piece of work too then, is he?' she asked.

'You could say that! He nicked Rhodri's bike last week and threw it in the canal. He tried to steal mine too, but he couldn't unlock it,' Charlie said. 'And you remember those chocolate cakes you made me for my birthday? He took them: scoffed the lot, right in front of me. At least Snitters gave him extra Maths homework too.'

'They're normally horribly insecure people, bullies.' Auntie said, picking a tea towel from the rail above the oven. 'Tell you what, when you go upstairs and see your uncle up in the greenhouse, I'm sure he'll be able to tell you a thing or two about circles. Maybe you could teach Mrs Snitterborne something.'

'Yeah, that'd be great. Teach the old bag a lesson!'

'I'm not sure you should call her that. She is still your teacher, even if she is an old dragon. Before you go upstairs, could you collect a basket of eggs from the Red Barn? I want to make some cakes, and whilst you're in there, make sure the chickens haven't started your uncle's old car.'

Charlie picked up a basket from beside the door.

'Oh, and don't forget to put some bait in the traps, for the rats,' Auntie called after him.

Charlie turned around and caught sight of her mimicking the action of someone loading a rifle and shooting it out of the window.

*

As he rushed around the inside of the barn picking up eggs from inside the old car, he couldn't help wondering why his uncle had let it get so scruffy and worn-out. He imagined what it must have looked like it in its original, gleaming condition, before so many of its parts had been taken for spares. What would it have been like before the seats and windscreen had been removed? He spotted the hole in the dashboard where the rev counter his uncle had fitted to his bike had once lived; it was loosely stuffed with straw and feathers. Could the Drakepuddle chickens have any idea how privileged they were? Probably not, he thought. Even though it was propped up on old bricks, not many chickens had their own Rolls Royce. And, Charlie noticed, they did seem to rather enjoy pecking at the buttons on the radio to change the music.

*

He placed the eggs on the table and sprinted up the winding staircase leading to the first floor. What invention would his uncle be working on? It had to be something incredible. It always was.

He climbed the second flight, a spiral staircase wrapped around a fireman's pole, which started at the top floor in the Ideas Room and reached all the way down to a bedroom on the ground floor.

He emerged in the huge, bright attic. It had so many large windows that, just as Auntie always said, it was like being in a greenhouse high in the air. Charlie liked to imagine, instead, that he was hanging in the observation deck of an old airship, floating over the countryside.

On a raised platform in the centre of the room, Uncle was busy at his desk. He had an old brass bar with his name engraved in fancy letters: *Peregrine Angstrom Clunckle. Inventor.* Both Charlie and Poppy had struggled to say *Uncle Peregrine* when they were younger. So whenever they had gone to visit, it was to see Auntie Chloe and *Uncle Clunckle,* at least until they were old enough to call him Uncle Pip.

'Mmm, a bit more, I think,' Uncle was saying to himself. He scribbled something on a notepad and replaced the pencil into the clip on the side of his spectacles.

the corner of the room interrupted, crackling loudly like an old gramophone. 'Sandwiches. Front garden,' Auntie's voice announced.

'Come on, Charlie. We don't want to keep Auntie waiting.' He checked his watch. 'It's lunch o'clock!'

It only took Uncle a few paces to reach the fireman's pole, from where he disappeared through the floor. Doris' ears pricked up. She leapt out of her basket and sprinted towards the wall and launched herself at a picture of a rabbit, which was glued onto a cat flap. Moments later, through the still-swinging door, Charlie could hear her barking as she slid down the laundry chute towards the kitchen.

Charlie waited for a light next to the pole to change from red to amber, then to green, and finally to purple, before he knew it was safe to follow.

*

As always, Uncle was the first to finish eating and excuse himself after lunch. When Charlie followed a few minutes later, something made him skid to a halt as he ran along the landing on the first floor. He stood motionless at the foot of the spiral staircase, unable to move. It was as if the object on the stairs was some kind of barrier commanding him to stop.

What was *that* doing there?

Charlie recognized the tidy handwriting at once. The neat way the words were arranged on the postcard seemed to match the way the card was resting on the stairs. It was exactly in the centre of the very first step, and it was leaning so that the address and message were angled directly towards him.

21

6

Uncle looked up from his desk through a huge magnifying glass attached to a white crash helmet. His eye looked as big as a grapefruit.

'Blinkin' fish, Charlie.' In one hand he was holding a surgeon's scalpel and in the other, a pair of tweezers. 'The bit of the fish what makes you brainy is near the fin on the back, but it's quite tiny, ever so fiddly. And fish don't just make you brainy. If you eat the right bit, you develop all sorts of abilities. That's why it's such a crucial ingredient.'

Charlie looked down at his uncle's desk. A large, colourful and very detailed diagram covered most of it. Other than some big capital letters, which read IQ-C_2 at the top, he couldn't read any of the scruffy writing.

'Abilities?' he asked. 'What sort of abilities?'

'Well, it sharpens your brain up, whatever situation you're in. That's the clever bit: it tunes itself to your surroundings. The problem is, the bit that boosts your brain is terrible hard to find, and you need to mix it with dried sprout extract, tomato seeds, cabbage chlorophyll, turnip tips, seaweed and about twenty other ingredients to boost it up enough for the formula to work. Tell you what though, if you leave it like that, it don't half taste flippin' horrible! This formula makes it taste just like custard he'd used to steal it from his uncle's Ideas Room. He placed it carefully into his school bag, next to his Maths book.

10

Less than twenty miles away, the Hunter sat in front of a desk. On it there was a shiny, silver cylinder.

Beads of sweat had broken out on the man's brow, making his blistered skin wet and clammy. He pushed his glasses back up his nose and ran his fingers over the stolen weapon.

Getting the Confogumist had been easy. He'd managed to get into the underground vault without any real difficulty, even though it had been so many years since he'd worked there. He'd fooled the security system into thinking that he was one of the security guards doing a routine check.

Of course, he knew that the really dangerous weapons were kept elsewhere, in some other secret place. Sooner or later he'd go looking for them too, but right now all he cared about was turning this crude prototype into something he could use to escape; somewhere to hide if he needed to.

He lowered a tube inside the open neck of the cylinder and took a moment to reflect on his own brilliance: breaking into one of the most secure vaults anywhere and stealing one of the Ministry's top-secret prototypes, one that he'd helped to design all those years before; and he'd stolen it in such a way that nobody would even notice it was gone. Genius!

It was a shame there was no one else to witness his cunning artistry, but he didn't care much for the company of other people. He was alone, with a handful of his other creations.

He flicked a switch and the machinery started to operate. The whirring pumps quietly sucked the contents from the cylinder and started reproducing them in the huge canisters lined up in neat rows in the neighbouring room.

He turned around and looked up at the pale, lifeless faces behind him. 'Not a bad day's work eh, my little angels, for a *dead* man!'

11

Charlie sat with Rhodri and Toby in their usual spot for lunch. He was fed up of his mum fussing over whether he'd eaten all his sprouts and carrots, or whether he was drinking enough horrible, warm water to help him concentrate, so they were out of sight of the counter where she worked, serving up the meals.

'Have you learnt that number Snitters asked you?' Toby asked as he moved his dinner plate to one side.

'My uncle gave me a great way of remembering it.' Charlie put his knife and fork down and shoved his pudding to the side. 'Wait till you see this.'

'Here comes Allsop and the heavies,' Toby said.

'Wonder whose dinner money he's nicked today,' added Rhodri.

Allsop strutted around the dinner hall, leaving a trail of spilt drinks and spluttering children.

'I hope he nudges me,' said Rhodri. 'I'll spill my drink right over his trousers. He'll look like he's wet himself.'

Charlie glanced around, lifted his school bag and, from the side pocket, he removed the small brick-shaped package and unwrapped it from the handkerchief. He fumbled and the carton slid across the floor.

He turned around to pick it up. 'My uncle gave me something that will show Snitterbor—'

It was the wrong moment. He tried to grab the package, but it was too late.

'What's that, Crump? Something for me?' Allsop said, scanning the dinner hall to make sure he was getting an audience.

Allsop's sidekicks, Boris Chugg and Griffith Blott, gaped at each other as if they weren't sure whether they were supposed to laugh or not.

'Er no. It's just custard, home-made.'

'I'll have it. I'll be doing you a favour. Your mum's cooking stinks! And you owe me for the extra Maths homework,' Allsop said, sneering in the direction of the serving counter.

'She didn't make it.'

'Even better! Your auntie must've made it. Those chocolate cakes she made — Remember? The ones you *gave* me? — they were nice enough.' Allsop snatched the packet from Charlie's hand and stuffed it into his pocket.

Before Charlie could get to his feet, Allsop pushed him hard in the chest with both hands, knocking the wind out of him. A whistle blew and the dinner hall became totally quiet.

Mr Rutherford put the whistle back in his pocket. He pointed at Allsop and then to his own eyes.

Allsop fixed Charlie with a look that dared him to stare back, before turning around and walking away.

Charlie didn't say anything. He stared at his jam tart and held his hands tight against his stomach, trying to soothe the painful dull ache.

'Why did you let him take it from you?' Rhodri asked.

'Yeah, you should stand up to him,' Toby added.

*

That afternoon, Mrs Snitterborne's class was interrupted by a knock on the door.

'Enter,' she announced, in a high-pitched screech.

Mr Merryweather, the headmaster, walked into the classroom followed by another man.

'Good afternoon, Mrs Snitterborne. Good afternoon class. This is Mr Tote. He is a reporter for *The Bugle* and he would like to take some photographs of our pupils in a classroom, for a piece he's writing about our school. Mrs Snitterborne has very kindly agreed that this class may be used.'

Mr Tote nodded towards the children and grunted.

Charlie had seen the man a few minutes before, parking his small, dirty van in one of the disabled parking bays, denting the car next to him whilst opening his door to empty the contents of an ashtray onto the floor.

Mrs Snitterborne seemed to have given herself a few extra squirts of perfume and was wearing the brightest red lipstick that Charlie had ever seen, as well as a pair of huge, shiny, dangly earrings.

'Now, class, we are all privileged and honoured to have such a splendid opportunity to demonstrate what a fine teaching establishment our school is, to a respected member of the journalistic profession.'

Charlie looked at Rhodri and then Toby. They were clearly as puzzled as he was by the ridiculous way Mrs Snitterborne was speaking.

'Haaacchh, haaacchh, ahaaaacchh, aaaaacchhhem!' She studied her handkerchief from different angles before returning it to its home inside the sleeve of her cardigan. Charlie noticed Mr Tote flinch

'I will let one of our star pupils demonstrate the mathematical qualities of one of nature's most wonderful geometric delights. Who would like to go first?'

She paused, looking around the classroom with her head tilted slightly higher than usual towards the ceiling.

'Tristan, I believe you had your hand up. Would you like to come and write, on the board, a property which describes a square?'

Tristan slid his chair back and walked to the front of the class. He had forgotten to raise his hand, so he did it after he'd stood up then realized this was a silly thing to do, so put it back down again, but not until he was nearly at the front of the class.

Mrs Snitterborne looked at the reporter. 'One of our star pupils,' she said.

The man from the newspaper responded with another

grunt.

She took the handkerchief out of the sleeve of her cardigan, licked it and wiped some jam off Tristan's cheek, replacing it with a lot of smudged lipstick instead. Charlie was glad Mrs Snitterborne wasn't *his* mum.

He glanced at Mr Tote, who was pretending to look through the viewfinder of his camera but really seemed more interested in reading a newspaper about horses.

Tristan picked up the marker and wrote, in very neat writing on the whiteboard: *A SQUARE HAS FOUR EQUAL SIDES AND FOUR RIGHT ANGLES.*

He put the marker pen down and was about to walk back to his desk when he turned back to the whiteboard and wrote the number *1* in front of his sentence. The shutter clicked on Mr Tote's camera. He hadn't meant to take a photograph, but he hadn't been concentrating and he seemed to be falling asleep.

'Excellent work, Tristan. Now who else would like to state a property of a square?'

Without waiting to be asked, Tristan turned around and wrote: *2. IT IS A TYPE OF RHOMBUS.*

Then he placed the marker on Mrs Snitterborne's table and went to sit down.

From a corner near the back, Jasper Allsop thrust his hand into the air.

'Internal angles summing to 360 degrees, 4 lines of symmetry. All squares are rhombi, but not all rhombi are squares,' he called out.

Charlie caught Rhodri's eye. The pair exchanged puzzled glances again, then looked back towards Mrs Snitterborne.

'Er, very good Jasper, er … Tristan was just coming to that, weren't you?'

'No, Mu— Mrs Snitterborne. That wasn't on the list of …'

Before he could finish his sentence, Mrs Snitterborne interrupted. *'And* who can tell me anything about *triangles?'*

'Three vertices. Internal angles summing to 180 degrees. Isosceles: two sides of equal length. Equilateral; all sides of equal length. Scalene; no sides of equal length. Obtuse: one angle greater than …' Allsop's hand was so high in the air it was pulling him out of his seat. He grunted and bit down on his lip. Charlie noticed the whole class were gawping at Allsop. There was something else strange too. Somehow, Charlie felt he knew what Allsop was going to say, before he said it.

'Yes, yes, we all, er … I mean, we all know, er … I mean … very good, Jasper,' said Mrs Snitterborne.

'Ahem. Now, Charlie. Do you remember the little task I set you about circles? Are you able to recite the value of Pi to ten decimal places?'

'No, Miss,' Charlie said, accidentally knocking his pencil case to the floor, where it smashed open and sent his pens and pencils rolling across the floor.

'As I expected,' she said, beaming at Mr Tote. 'Some of our pupils do not take education as seriously as they should. Such a shame that not all young children can appreciate the mathematical beauty that lies within everyday geometry. Even the *finest* teacher cannot tutor an ignoramus. Now, Tristan, perhaps you could be so kind?'

Charlie stood up from his chair. 'Not ten decimal

places,' he said. 'I can do it to *fifteen* though.' He shot a quick sideways glimpse at Rhodri before continuing. 'Three point one four one five nine two six five three five eight nine seven nine three.' The words flowed more easily than he'd expected. He hadn't even used the poem.

'Well, um ...very good. Er ... Tristan was just about to —'

'Hnnnng!' Allsop bit down on his lip again 'What are those pretty silver things, mmmmm?' He looked scared, as if he had no idea why the words were coming out of his mouth?

Was this what Uncle's invention did to people? Charlie thought.

Mr Tote put his camera down and picked up his note-pad.

'Two three ... *hnnnng* ... eight ... *hnnng* ... yummy.' Allsop's confused face carried on. 'Four ... Help! ... six ... Bet they taste nice, I NEED THE TOILET!' Then, with his eyes bulging, he suddenly stopped talking.

Charlie heard someone gasp. There was a wet patch starting to grow at the front of Allsop's trousers.

Mr Tote quickly located the video camera in his scruffy brown bag and removed the lens cap.

'Two ... six. I've wet my pants. OH NO!' As he continued to babble away, he started to snake towards the front of the class, slowly at first, then more quickly, darting this way and that. Suddenly he hid beneath one of the desks.

'Jasper, what are you doing?' Mrs Snitterborne asked. Charlie detected more than a hint of panic in her voice. 'Get back to your desk! Sit down at once!' She wasn't speaking with the funny accent any more.

Allsop crawled out from under the desk and walked towards the front of the class. He was staring at Mrs Snitterborne.

'SIT DOWN AT ONCE!' she demanded again.

It was as if he couldn't hear her. His bulging eyes stared at her face as he inched towards her. He jerked forwards as if he was about to kiss her on the cheek, but instead, he lunged towards her right ear and grabbed her shiny, silver earring between his teeth. Charlie felt his cheeks burn. This *had* to be the IQ-C$_2$ causing Allsop to behave so weirdly.

'Get off, you beast!' She tried to push her attacker away. There was no way that Allsop was going to let go. He looked like he couldn't. The fastener came off the back of Mrs Snitterborne's earring and the entire class gasped as Allsop swallowed it whole.

12

'What a day!' Rhodri said. 'What made Allsop some kind of Maths genius all of a sudden?'

'Dunno,' Charlie replied, rummaging around inside his school bag.

'Oh, you never got round to telling me about that thing at lunchtime. What was it?'

'Oh, nothing.'

'Yes, it was. You said "wait till you see this".'

'Oh, it was just, er, nothing.' There was no way Charlie was going to explain about the IQ-C$_2$. Not after what had happened to Allsop.

Charlie tipped the contents of his bag onto his bedroom floor. The lid came off his broken pencil case and his pens and pencils rolled everywhere again.

'What's that?' Rhodri asked.

It was the postcard. It must have fallen back into Charlie's bag when he'd fumbled with the package at lunchtime.

Rhodri picked it up and looked at the picture. 'Flying Fish Cove? Where's that?' He flicked it over and started to read it. He looked up at Charlie with a puzzled expression. 'Why have you got a postcard addressed to the Ministry of Defence?'

'My uncle gave it to me.'

'Your uncle? Why did *he* have a postcard addressed to the—?'

'It's all a bit weird. The card wasn't addressed to him. It was for GB. That's Godfrey Blessings from the village where he lives, and there's been a break-in. I don't know what it's all about. There's a code in the message.'

'A code? What kind of code?'

'The capital letters spell *breach*. There's been a breach of some kind and I heard my uncle talking about a group called the Minatauri and someone called Flack, whoever he is, or *was*. Apparently he's dead. The breach, whatever it is, could put everyone at risk.'

'"Everyone at risk?" What do you mean by that?'

'I don't know. *Everyone* and *everything,* he said.'

Rhodri studied the card again. 'Well, if your uncle's

got someone else's postcard and there's been some kind of breach at the Ministry of Defence, do you think we should do something.'

'Like what?' Charlie said.

'I think we should look up Flying Fish Cove.' Rhodri said.

*

'What sort of *incident*?' asked Mr Crump, removing his tie later that evening as he settled down to watch the end of the local news.

'A pretty weird one!' replied Charlie. 'Jasper Allsop started running around the classroom talking gobbledygook, then he attacked Mrs Snitterborne!'

'*Gobbledygook?* What *kind* of gobbledygook?'

'Well, er, the Maths kind,' replied Charlie.

'That boy has never been right; always a troublemaker. I knew his father from when he worked at the Egg Board. He wasn't much better; always mucking about. I was his manager when he got sacked for throwing eggs around.'

'Look, Dad, it's on the news,' Charlie interrupted. 'Mum, come and look. Our school is on the news!'

Mum and Poppy ran into the living room.

'I was lucky enough to be an eyewitness to this bizarre incident.' Charlie recognized the scruffy reporter holding a microphone as the same man who had been in his classroom earlier that day.

'It was an early closure for Allsford School today, after a pupil attacked a teacher and ate some of her jewellery.'

The newsreader butted in. 'I'm sorry, Geoffrey. It sounded a bit like you said he "*ate some of her jewellery*".'

'Yes, that's right, some earrings, her car keys and a brooch. We think it was of a bee ... or a dragonfly. It was a tug of war between the boy and the earrings, and eventually the boy won.'

'Oh, I see. Is there any news on the teacher?'

The reporter looked down at his notepad for a second before returning to the camera. 'She was clearly shocked by the incident, having worked at the school for over ten years, and nothing like this ever happening before. The headteacher has said they're treating the assault as an isolated event and possibly the result of exam stress ... or some kind of allergic reaction.'

'Not like the school dinners I remember, Geoffrey! It was lumpy mash and limp salad when I was a boy, not keys and brooches. Anyway, on to the weather forecast. Will the sunshine continue, Kat?'

Charlie felt himself going red as his mother and father's gazes settled on him.

13

Someone else had seen the news report too.

The Hunter's assistant had sat patiently through hours of TV news clips, scanning dozens of channels on a large bank of screens and monitors, just as she had been taught. Something caught her attention: a few words triggered something in her memory: *attacked ... war ... assault ... allergic reaction ...*

She had replayed the news item to her master. He had been pleased. Very pleased.

The Hunter picked up a telephone. 'We can get to him through the boy. It looks like he's taken some kind of untested additive. It could have potential. Who else could have come up with something so flawed and think it would be a good idea to test it on a child? Check out that ramshackle old farm. There may be other stuff in there. Leave the boy to me. I know exactly how I'm going to get to him.'

The Hunter hung up. He looked at the frozen image on his screen — a scruffy-looking reporter, wearing a long, dirty, brown coat. 'I know someone who's going to lead me to him.'

14

Mrs Crump stood in the hallway with the telephone in her hand.

'Yes, I totally understand. Yes, he most certainly *is* here.'

Charlie had a very good idea who she was speaking to, and what it was about.

'We'll speak to him about it first,' she continued. 'No pocket money for at *least* a fortnight. No, he must learn his lesson. Yes, of course.' She turned to Charlie, 'We'll have to think about it. Okay, see you later.'

She put the telephone down and scowled at Charlie.

'That was your uncle. He saw the bit about your school on the local news and says that he thinks *you* might have something to do with that terrible incident between Jasper Allsop and Mrs Snitterborne; that you might have taken something from his place at the weekend.' She placed her hands on her hips. 'Well? Did you?'

It was pointless pretending he knew nothing about the missing parcel, 'But Allsop stole it from me!' he pleaded.

'It's totally unacceptable to take things without permission from anyone, especially your uncle! We're stopping your pocket money for starters and he's coming over tonight to see your father. You'd better have a good apology for him.'

Charlie knew when he was in trouble. The pocket money was no problem — he'd been saving it for the summer holidays anyway — but what did she have to think about? It couldn't be stopping him from going to Drakepuddle, could it? No way! That would be so unfair! Just because he'd taken a packet of sludge out of a rubbish bin? How would he tell Rhodri?

*

Later that evening, from his bedroom, he heard the distinctive noise of his father's car pull on to the driveway. Doris was standing on Uncle's lap with her head sticking out of the passenger's window. She jumped out of the window before Mr Crump had turned the engine off.

Charlie watched his uncle remove a large holdall from the boot. He could just about make out the voices from his bedroom window.

'I hope you have more luck programmin' it than I

have,' he heard Uncle say. 'Bloomin' thing almost had me downside-up halfway to Timbuktu on Tuesday.'

Charlie could just about read the distinctive writing on the holdall's label. It was the recognizable curly text and logo of the engineering firm that Uncle used for making some of his prototypes.

Nothing ever came out of a QT Fitchett bag that wasn't incredible in some way.

'Charlie, come downstairs at once!' Mum shouted.

Poppy was waiting for him in the hallway. She moved her finger across her neck to mimic the action of someone having their throat cut.

Charlie moped into the dining room where his mum was pouring three cups of tea. There were five plates on the table.

'Well, Charlie, what have you got to say to your uncle?' Mrs Crump asked.

'Sorry, Uncle.'

'And?' his mother added.

'I promise not to take anything from your Ideas Room without asking again.'

'Too right you won't! No pocket money for two weeks! No bike for a while either. We're also seriously considering whether you should even be allowed to go and stay with your uncle, after such a terrible betrayal of trust,' his father said.

Charlie had a terrible feeling in his stomach, even worse than when Allsop had knocked the wind out of him. It was like it was twisted in a dozen very tight knots. Poppy kicked him under the table. He ignored her. He couldn't lift his head and he couldn't help wondering how

45

much worse it would have been if *he'd* been the one that had attacked Snitterborne.

Eventually, Uncle spoke.

'Never mind. Apology accepted. One o' nine lives, eh! That batch were a bad 'un. All the components got mixed up, so it were bound to have some side effects. Anyway, I reckon them two deserved it.' Uncle chuckled. 'That recipe would be perfect for some uses, eh? Could turn people into a load of jibberin' idiots, or scaredy-cats. I could call it 'Cowardy Custard!' Heh heh!' He nudged Charlie with his elbow. 'Cowardy Custard!'

Charlie noticed his father pretending to cough, desperately trying to hide the fact that he was laughing.

Soon, the whole family had caught the laughing bug. Even Doris was running around the table, chasing her tail, barking and howling excitedly.

Uncle was the first to stop laughing. 'Anyhow,' he said, 'if you could reprogram the voice control of the apparatus, I'd be very grateful. Q's done a great job of buildin' it, but it needs someone who speaks proper. It don't recognize half my words.'

That wasn't surprising. Charlie knew Uncle often mis-pronounced words and his spelling was terrible. He watched him take a piece of paper from inside the top pocket of his shirt. He unfolded it and slid it across the table to Mr Crump.

'Here's the instructions. Hopefully it all makes sense.'

'What is the invention, Uncle?' Charlie interrupted.

'Oh my giddy aunt, Charlie,' Uncle replied. 'You *are* keen to get through them nine lives, ain't you!' He tapped his nose and looked over the top of his spectacles at

Charlie.

'Yes, don't you think your curiosity has got you into enough trouble for one day?' Charlie's father added, reaching towards the piece of paper.

Although, from his side of the table, the writing was upside-down, Charlie could just about read most of the words. He placed his elbows on the table and started rubbing his forehead.

'What's wrong, Charlie?' his mother asked.

'Oh, er, I've just got a bit of a headache,' Charlie lied.

He started to read the badly spelled instructions to him-self. When he looked up, Uncle was glaring at him with a most extraordinary expression on his face, scowling at Charlie ... yet somehow, he was smiling too.

15

He'd been sent to bed early. As he lay under his duvet, trying to make sense of his bicycle handbook by torch-light, Charlie overheard Uncle in the hallway downstairs.

'I'll just say goodnight to Charlie and Poppy, then I'd best get back to Drakepuddle.' When he heard the stairs creaking, Charlie switched off his torch. His door opened and Uncle walked inside.

'I'll be off now then, Charlie. Promise me you won't muck about with the equipment in that bag. It's dangerous in the wrong hands.'

'I won't,' Charlie replied.

'You sure? You seem terrible curious about it. I saw you tryin' to read the instructions.'

'Sorry, it's just, all your inventions are so ...'

'*Dangerous!*' Uncle interrupted.

Charlie sat up. 'What do you mean?'

'There's summat you should know about my inventions, Charlie.' Uncle's eyes gazed around the room before settling on the postcard. It was still on the floor near Charlie's bed. 'But before I tell you, I want you to understand that sometimes ... well, you can't always choose what you're good at.'

What did he mean by that? Charlie thought.

Uncle paused for a moment before he continued. 'I see you've still got that card. Godfrey was asking where it had got to. Perhaps I should take it back.'

'Oh, by the way, Rhodri and me looked up Christmas Island. We couldn't find out much about it, But we did find out they did some kind of weapons testing there, a long time ago.'

'That's true.' Uncle nodded. For a moment, it looked like he couldn't think of what to say next. 'You remember you worked out what the message said?'

'It said "breach".' Charlie spelled out the letters too, as if to emphasize the way the word had been hidden within the message. *But I didn't work it out; you told me.*

'And you know what *breach* means?'

'It means, well, like a break-in, or a leak.'

'It does mean that, but ... '

'But what?'

'If I tell you, you must promise me that you can keep a secret.'

'Of course, I can,' he said. Although he knew that it was probably already too late for that.

'BREACH means ... well, it's what's called an acronym: the letters stand for summat; like SCUBA. The fella that sent that card weren't goin' SCUBA divin' – he couldn't even swim! I forget what SCUBA stands for, but I'll never forget what BREACH stands for.'

Uncle must have read the expression on Charlie's dimly-lit face.

'I knew your curiosity would get the better of you,' he said, 'BREACH, Charlie, stands for *Battlefield-Related Evaluation and Analysis of Concepts and Hardware.* That was my department ... at the Ministry.'

'What? Weapons and stuff?' Charlie's mind started racing.

'Like I said, Charlie, sometimes you can't choose the things you're good at. I've been involved with some right monstrosities over the years. Thankfully most of 'em are safely under lock and key, where no one can find 'em.' He turned to leave. 'Sorry,' he said.

'Wait,' Charlie said. 'What about the Minatauri? What have they got to do with it?'

Uncle turned around and walked back into Charlie's room. He let out a long sigh. 'They've always tried to get hold of the latest stuff — weapons — no matter what the cost. They made me what I am, Charlie.'

'They made you *what you are?*'

'The reason I'm ... It's because ... because of what they did. They ...' He let out another sigh.

'They what?'

'They killed my parents, Charlie. I was seven.'

He left the room and Charlie heard his bedroom door click shut.

16

It was the last day of term and Charlie dragged himself, yawning to the special assembly. It was the last one of the school year. He hadn't slept well, as there had been so many thoughts flying around his mind. He knew that his uncle had been orphaned and now he knew how; the Minatauri had killed his parents. But why? And what about the contraption in that bag? Might it be some kind of secret weapon? Was his father involved in the whole thing? Had he really lost one of his nine lives, like Uncle had said? How many lives had he *really* lost?

He sat down next to Rhodri who was trying to get his attention. He seemed to be nodding towards the stage. Charlie looked. What was Snitterborne doing back at school? His mother had said she wouldn't be coming back before the end of term, but there she was, on the stage with the other teachers, hiding near the back, with her chin held low and moving only her eyes, never her head. She slowly scanned the room.

'I thought Snitters was in the looney bin!' Dylan Hodson whispered to Charlie.

'I heard she'd gone totally bonkers and had to have her food all mushed up,' Toby added.

Her pale face winced when she first caught sight of

50

Allsop walking into the hall.

Rhodri gave Charlie a gentle nudge with his elbow. 'Have you seen Snitters? She looks like she's seen a ghost,' he whispered.

'Yeah, either that or someone's tried to eat her keys again!' joked Toby.

As more of the pupils followed Mrs Snitterborne's horrified stare towards Allsop, Charlie overheard all sorts of rumours start to spread.

'Have you heard? Allsop was sent to a special prison where he had to be tied to a post! They had to feed him keys and watches with a giant robot arm! He even tried to eat that!'

'Yeah, I know, and he has to sleep sitting on a toilet too!'

'And people with clipboards were watching him the whole time!'

Charlie smiled uneasily, but kept very quiet.

Mr Merryweather walked onto the stage holding a large bundle of papers. The whispers started to fade, the teachers stopped chatting and the room gradually fell into silence.

Charlie could see ribbons overflowing from the side of a bowl. It must contain medals. Next to the bowl there were ten or so trophies of various shapes and sizes. Charlie knew there'd be no trophy or medal for him.

'This has been a very *eventful* year for our school,' Mr Merryweather began. There was some muttering and sub- dued laughter from the teachers on the stage. 'But I'm very pleased to say that we have had a great number of academic successes, with pupils achieving record pass rates.' Mr Merryweather paused, and turned his head to face the teachers behind him. He removed his hands from the pedestal and started to clap. The pupils clapped too and the teachers nodded and smiled, apart from Mrs Snitterborne.

As Mr Merryweather's speech continued, Charlie's mind drifted off into a daydream. He imagined he was in a laboratory with his uncle. They were wearing white lab coats and carrying clipboards. In the centre of the laboratory, Allsop was chained to a huge metal seat, which had bite-marks on the legs. He had his back to Charlie.

Charlie had a large broom handle with a fork tied to the end. On the end of the fork there was a huge, hot, steaming sausage. They carefully lowered the fork in front of Allsop, who jerked and starting making grunting and grumbling sounds.

Charlie and his uncle started to write notes on their clipboards.

'I'll get you for this!' Allsop snarled, leaning towards the sausage. He bit into it and flicked his head to the side, throwing the sausage to the floor, then lunged forward to take a bite out of the fork. There was a dreadful crunch.

'Interestin', very interestin'!' Uncle was saying.

Charlie nodded. 'Yes, interesting. Very …'

Suddenly, Allsop turned around. Only it wasn't his face anymore. It was Charlie who was sitting on the chair, and a trickle of drool was dribbling down his chin.

It wasn't a daydream either. Charlie had fallen asleep. He snorted and woke suddenly, jerking his head.

Mr Merryweather and almost all of the teachers were

looking at him. As he wiped his mouth, he realized that nearly everyone else was staring at him too.

Mr Merryweather continued. 'I don't want to dwell on recent events but it is a timely reminder that we have rules for a purpose. Do *NOT* take things which don't belong to you.'

17

It seemed so unfair that Maths was the final lesson on the very last day of term. All of the other teachers had let their pupils bring things in to share with their classmates.

Mr Stilton had allowed the pupils to take their favourite records in to his music class. Poppy had, of course, taken some dreadful song by her favourite band, the Sense-it-ifs. Charlie, along with every other boy at the school, absolutely hated the sound of Declan O'Duff's voice.

Mr Rutherford had a selection of funny quotes inside a hat, and let his class each pick one and read it in any style they liked.

Mrs Snitterborne usually made her class listen to her describe her favourite formula and then look for an example over the summer of how that formula could be used to describe something incredibly boring.

As he sat, willing the school day to end, Charlie could feel Allsop's stare fixing into the back of his head, like a hawk focusing on its prey.

He tried not to think about what Allsop might be scheming. Instead, he tried to concentrate on his own plans. Rhodri had told him that he would be dropped off at the Crump's house at nine o' clock on Sunday morning with his bike and rucksack. Charlie kept that thought in his mind as he watched Mrs Snitterborne. She seemed to be shaking slightly as she replaced her handkerchief inside her sleeve.

She surveyed the class and when she spoke, her voice was quieter than it had been before 'The Incident'. Charlie noticed that she wasn't wearing any jewellery.

'In light of ... ahem ... recent events, it would be more appropriate for you all to work quietly through the end-of-year progress test and a series of extra computations than for me to thrill you all with my formula stories. There will be no need to talk. The papers should keep you occupied until the end of the lesson. Most of you will be unable to complete all of the tasks in the time allowed, so you will have to finish the rest of the paper over the holiday. Does anybody have any questions?'

'Yes, Mrs Snitterborne. When may we give you our cards and presents?' asked Florence.

'Well, how lovely! You may of course bring them to me now.' Mrs Snitterborne folded her arms and seemed to be trying to smile. She mumbled something under her breath but Charlie couldn't hear what it was. Her shoulders shuddered and she looked at the floor. After a few seconds, she turned to the window and began to make a strange, babbling, laughing noise.

Several of the children pushed their chairs back cautiously and rummaged through their bags. Four or five stood up with their thank-you gifts and cards.

Mrs Snitterborne snapped her head to face the class. 'But I do NOT like apples. No one has brought apples, have they?'

Molly Jones sat down again. Charlie noticed her freckled face trying to conceal a mixture of disappoint-ment and embarrassment as she tried to hide something in her school bag without anyone noticing.

Florence, Tristan and a couple of the other children made their way to the front of the class with their thank-you cards and gifts. They'd all returned to their desks when Allsop stood up and started creeping slowly to-wards the front of the class with a piece of paper in his hand. He held his head low, avoiding eye contact with anyone. Whispers broke out around the classroom. Allsop had never given any teacher a thank-you card.

'What's he doing?' Rhodri mouthed to Charlie.

Charlie shrugged.

Mrs Snitterborne took a couple of steps backwards and placed her hands behind her back, searching for the wall.

'Er … Jasper,' Her voice sounded strange and squeaky. 'Slow down, Jasper,' she added. 'In fact, you can leave your card on your desk and I'll collect it at the end.' She seemed to blurt the last few words of her sentence out extremely quickly.

Allsop mumbled something. It was difficult to hear, even for Charlie, and Allsop was standing right next to him.

He continued shuffling towards the front of the class, never taking his eyes off the front of his shoes or the floor. He muttered something again.

'Pardon?' said Mrs Snitterborne.

Allsop didn't look up. He repeated himself. This time Charlie could just about make out what he was saying.

'S'not a card.'

'I'm ... er ... sorry, Jasper, could you speak up, please. I can hardly hear you.'

'S'not a card, Miss,' he repeated a little louder, still looking at the floor. 'I've finished the test.'

'What? Imposs— Oh, er ... leave it on your desk ... er ...'

'Got this for you too,' he mumbled, putting his hand into his trouser pocket and removing an untidy handkerchief that was wrapped up to make a small bundle.

Mrs Snitterborne tried to focus on the package. She looked up at Allsop's face. He was still staring at his shoes, shuffling forwards. Her attention fell onto the package in his hands and her narrow-eyed squint suddenly changed into an expression of total horror, like someone had just opened a box of deadly snakes in front of her. She let out a gasp, almost tripping as she stepped backwards towards the wall.

Her face had turned as white as a sheet of paper.

'It's your earrings and keys, Miss. They came out the other end,' Allsop muttered.

Still looking at the floor, with his outstretched hands holding the package and his test paper, for once, Allsop didn't seem to enjoy being the focus of attention for so many of his classmates.

18

It was a perfect day for cycling, with only the very lightest of breezes and just a few clouds dotted around the sky. Charlie's father had suggested putting the bikes on the cycle rack and driving the boys to Drakepuddle Farm to save time, but Charlie had managed to persuade his parents that they needed the cycle ride to burn off the huge breakfast Mr Crump had cooked: *The Grand Slam* he called it. Anyway, Poppy still hadn't been ready when the boys had set off.

They were enjoying ducking and diving in and out of each other's slipstream, in time to the music blaring out of Charlie's handlebars.

'So you nicked something off your uncle?' Rhodri asked.

'It's supposed to make you smarter. I wanted to show Snitters.'

'But your uncle is a secret weapons inventor, and you nicked one of his inventions?'

'It was before I knew he was a weapons inventor. Anyway, shut up about that! You're not supposed to know.'

Charlie had hoped that admitting the truth to Rhodri would have made him feel better. Instead, he felt worse than ever.

They had got just past the village of Pudbury and were about to start off down the hill towards Great Disbury when Charlie's bike sounded a buzzer in response to the distinctive beeping of Mr Crump's car horn. The two boys pulled over to the side of the road and Charlie's music turned itself off.

The car windows were all open and Charlie could see the girls in the back seat, their hair blowing around in the wind.

Bryony waved at Charlie and Rhodri as they drove past. 'Yooo hooo!' she shouted.

Poppy had her thumb on the end of her nose and was waving her fingers and sticking her tongue out. The very recognizable high-pitched voices of the Sense-it-ifs screeching through the radio made Charlie cringe.

'Thank God I'm not in the car listening to that!' he said.

As the car disappeared down the hill, it became quiet and peaceful again. Only the sound of the birds singing, the distant chugging of a tractor and a slight hum from some nearby overhead power lines interrupted the silence.

'That's better. Peace and quiet again,' Rhodri said.

'That's odd. An alarm's just gone off on my bike computer. It's a weather warning,' Charlie said.

Rhodri tilted his head back. 'There's hardly a cloud in the sky. It can't possibly rain.'

'No, it's predicting fog! That can't be right. I'll mention it to my uncle. It's probably just a bug.' Charlie turned his music back on. 'Come on, let's go.'

'Wait! Can you smell that?' Rhodri asked. 'What a weird smell.'

'Nothing to do with me!'

'You sure?' Rhodri asked as he got onto his bike. 'You did have a second dollop of beans with your Grand Slam!'

The two boys headed off down the hill towards Great Disbury laughing.

They didn't notice the power lines above them start to buzz and crackle. They certainly didn't notice the red-hot glow of the cable against the blue sky, or the strange cloud of mist rolling in from the valley behind them.

19

Charlie and Rhodri cycled past the Pig and Whistle, where Uncle took part in the local pub quiz on Wednesday evenings. One of the villagers, who Charlie recognized as another friend of his uncle's, stepped out of an old telephone box on the village green. He lifted his cap and waved it. 'Morning, Charlie!' he said.

'Morning, Mr Twenny,' Charlie replied as they turned off the main road.

'Who's that?' Rhodri asked.

'It's just someone from my uncle's quiz team: *The Great Disbury Guardians*. He runs the chip shop.'

'Oh, right. Tell you what … It's all here, isn't it?' Rhodri said.

'What do you mean?' asked Charlie.

'Well, for a small village, there's a village shop, a pub,

a bakery, a chip shop, even a train station.'

'It's not much more than a platform really,' Charlie said. 'Only about one train an hour stops here. Have you really never been here before?'

'No. My dad always drives down the bypass. He says it's much quicker.'

As the boys pedalled past the Post Office, Charlie spotted Godfrey Blessings watering the hanging baskets outside. 'Morning,' he said.

'Morning, Charlie. Have a nice holiday,' Godfrey Blessings replied without turning around. 'Send me a postcard.'

'How did he know it was you?' Rhodri asked.

'Dunno. My uncle must've told him we were coming. It's a small village. Everyone seems to know everyone else's business here.'

'Why did he ask you to send him a postcard though?'

'I think he was just joking.' Charlie said, drawing alongside Rhodri. 'Don't forget, no one knows you've seen that one I showed you. I'm supposed to have kept it a secret. You'd better not mention it.'

'I think it's all weird.' Rhodri said.

'Why?'

'Well, if it was so secret, how come you ended up with it? And look at this place: some of the street names are really odd, the houses are all so old-fashioned, but they all have tons of aerials on the roof. And look at that hedge!'

Charlie had never really noticed the roofs before. The houses and cottages were mostly old stone and they all had pretty window boxes and small front gardens. But

Rhodri was right, there *did* seem to be an unusually large number of aerials of different shapes and sizes sticking out at funny angles from the crooked roofs. One house, in particular, an old, white cottage with a thatched roof, had so many aerials that it looked like they'd been dropped into the straw from a low-flying aeroplane. Amongst the selection of aerials, he could see one that was rotating slowly, like a small radar.

At least Charlie could explain why the hedge Rhodri had pointed out was trimmed into the shape of a large pig carrying a briefcase, and running away from a crowd of people.

'That house with the pig hedge belongs to Dorian Dobson, the famous artist. Last year the hedge was the Loch Ness Monster, with two heads, one at each end. And before that,' Charlie paused to change the mode of his bike, 'it was a big wedding cake.'

They cycled on for a few minutes, past the back of the village green. Charlie looked over his shoulder to have another look at the roofs. Strangely, most of the aerials had disappeared. He continued past the house with the unusually shaped hedge, and turned into the lane which led to Drakepuddle Farm. This was Charlie's favourite part of the journey; as he free-wheeled down the small hill, gaining speed towards the ford that crossed the lane, he felt the rush of air on his face. It always made him imagine he was an eagle swooping to pluck a fish out of a river, except that, unlike an eagle, he always stuck his legs out to the side so his feet wouldn't get wet.

Once he reached the farmhouse, Charlie locked his bike up against the front door and waited for Rhodri to catch up.

'Come on slow coach. Let's get unpacked,' Charlie said as Rhodri arrived.

Rhodri parked his bike next to Charlie's. He was obviously not quite so used to cycling up and down the hilly roads and lanes as Charlie. Then again, his bike didn't have the same features as Charlie's either.

There was a puzzled expression on Rhodri's face as he tried to catch his breath. 'Are you *sure,*' he said as he gulped in a couple of breaths, 'that your uncle's … *a genius?*' he wheezed.

Charlie followed Rhodri's gaze towards the handwritten sign hanging from the rusty nail: *PLEEZE DO NOT YUZE THIS DOR. YUZE THIS WON INSTEAD.*

Underneath the scruffy writing, there was an arrow pointing to the side of the house.

20

'What? The front door opens into a bedroom? And what's that?' Rhodri was gawping at the fireman's pole in the corner.

'It comes down from the attic,' Charlie explained. 'He says it's important to be able to get to bed quickly, when you're tired!'

'So he really *does* work up in the attic, then slide down a pole when he's tired, to get to bed?' Rhodri muttered. 'I thought you were just making that up.'

'Er, yeah, of course he does. Why would I make it up?' Charlie was spared any more of Rhodri's questions as a tractor chugged into the yard and stopped outside the door. Auntie slid elegantly off the seat and picked up her handbag, which had been hanging on a hook next to the steering wheel.

'Morning, boys. You must be Rhodri.' Auntie thrust her hand out to greet Rhodri. 'Very nice to meet you!' she said, shaking his hand vigorously. 'The girls are up in the sewing room. Poppy seems to think she hasn't packed enough clothes! Can you believe it? Three suitcases! Anyway, bring your rucksacks inside. You must be hungry too. I've got some cake on the go. You *do* like triple chocolate fudge wondercake, don't you, Rhodri?'

'Er, yeah,' Rhodri replied.

'Good. Your uncle will be back soon, Charlie.'

She walked back towards the door and lifted her hand to her forehead to shield her eyes from the sun and scanned the horizon. 'He can't have gone far. He knows you're coming before lunchtime.'

Having heard her tractor arrive, four of Auntie's cats had appeared from their various hiding places and were brushing against her legs, purring. She smiled at the boys. 'I can always call him on the radio if he's not back before lunch is ready. Come on, let's get those rucksacks in.'

Charlie and Rhodri followed Auntie through the kitchen and up the twisting staircase to the first floor.

There were three rooms on the right-hand side of the landing, all of which had signs on the door. The first was labelled *LOFT* and was largely full of junk, or at least, what appeared to be junk. In contrast to the piles of stacked boxes, there was a large four-poster bed against the wall next to a huge window, which was framed by frilly, blue curtains. There was also a bedside table with an alarm clock and a lamp neatly arranged on top of it.

'I thought you boys would be comfortable in here,' Auntie said, opening the door to the next room.

Rhodri read the sign on the door.

KUP OF TEA

'This is where he likes to come and read the paper,' Charlie began explaining to Rhodri, 'and have a—'

'Let me guess. Cup of tea?' Rhodri interrupted.

'Actually, he prefers coffee, but he says he couldn't spell that,' Charlie said.

Rhodri opened his mouth to speak. 'Actually ...' he started to say. Instead, he screwed his face up. 'Oh, never mind.'

'In you go, boys. Make yourselves at home.' Auntie held the door open.

'Wow! Look at that train set!' Rhodri said, pointing towards a large model railway, which was set up on a table next to the window.

'That's where you'll be sleeping, Rhodri, and you mustn't let Charlie's uncle hear you call it that! It's a *model railway.*'

'What? I'm sleeping on a *trainset?* Won't that be a bit ... well, uncomfortable?' Rhodri questioned.

'*Model railway!*' Auntie corrected as she walked over to the fireplace. 'Charlie knows how to turn it back into a bed, so we'll leave it as it is for now.' She rotated a small key on a clock, which was ticking on the mantelpiece. 'I've turned the chimes off. You don't want them keeping you awake all night, not with what we've got planned for tomorrow. Come on, boys, you can put your clothes in the *armoire* over there, if you need to.' She signalled to a very fancy wardrobe next to the fireplace. 'I'm going to have another look for your uncle. Oh, where on earth has he got to? It's twelve o'clock already!'

'Wow! What a great room!' Rhodri said, dragging his rucksack along the floor. 'Do you always sleep here when you come to visit?'

'Yeah,' Charlie replied. 'Cool, isn't it. I really like the view.'

Rhodri threw his rucksack onto a large leather sofa and looked out through the huge window.

'Wow! It's amazing. You can see the whole village. Is that the stream we cycled through?'

'Yeah, it is. I wonder where my uncle is. He must have bumped into one of his friends from the village.'

'Maybe he's designing some kind of secret weapon, or something?'

Charlie frowned at Rhodri. 'More likely he's chatting to someone in his quiz team. He spends ages nattering to them. Sometimes they go on for hours.'

21

'It's too late now for cake; it's nearly lunchtime. Where can he be?' Auntie said, reaching for some plates from a rack on the wall.

'Where did Uncle Pip say he was going?' asked Charlie.

'He didn't! He just said he'd be back by lunchtime. It's nearly one o'clock. I'll give him a call on the radio, in case he's got stuck somewhere.' She put the plates on the table and picked up a walkie-talkie from its charger in the corner of the kitchen. She twisted a knob on the top and the radio started hissing and crackling.

'Guardia— I mean can— oh, silly me. Mother Goose to Sparrow. Where are you? Over.'

There was a break in the static and the response sputtered back over the small radio.

'Shan't be long. On me way 'ome. Over.'

'But *where* are you? Over,' asked Auntie.

'Over the Pig and Whistle. Back soon. Over.'

'Did he say he was at the Pig and Whistle pub?' Charlie asked.

'Probably bumped into one of his friends from the quiz team, so you were right,' added Rhodri.

'No, he said he was *over* the Pig and Whistle. Shh, I think I can hear him now.'

Charlie concentrated. Above the noise of some cows mooing, he could hear a faint buzz, like the sound of a huge swarm of angry bees, and it seemed to be getting louder.

The crackling in Auntie's radio was interrupted again by Uncle's voice. 'Establishin' conditions. Over.'

As the buzzing got louder, Charlie and Rhodri looked up to try and see what was causing the strange rattling noise above their heads. The lights in the kitchen ceiling had begun shaking. Auntie hurried towards the plates on the table. They were clattering too, and sliding towards the edge. The whole room had started wobbling as if an earthquake was shaking it from side to side. Charlie and Rhodri ducked instinctively as the buzzing turned into a thunderous, whooshing roar.

Before Auntie could reach them, the plates shuffled over the edge of the table and smashed to the floor. Immediately, a dustpan and brush appeared from beneath one of the kitchen cupboards and started dealing with the breakages.

'Boys and their toys,' Auntie said.

Poppy and Bryony came running into the kitchen from upstairs.

'What was *that?*' yelled Poppy.

Through one of the kitchen windows, Charlie caught a tiny glimpse of a small, fast-moving aircraft, flying very low between the gaps of the farm buildings. He couldn't make out any detail before it disappeared behind a barn again. The tone of the engine changed as the aircraft turned back towards the farmhouse. He caught another glance through a different window. It looked like a very small helicopter. Charlie led the rush into the garden.

'I can't see it,' Rhodri said.

'Nor can I. It must be too low,' Charlie replied.'

Then, from behind the Red Barn, the machine reappeared. It whooshed low over their heads in a steep, fast turn and then disappeared behind the barn again. It looked like it was carrying two people. The Drakepuddle chickens scattered in every direction, having only just cautiously re-emerged from the barn, where they had fled the first time the machine had swooped overhead. Even

Nosebag, the farm donkey, had turned up to see what the commotion was all about; he sauntered into the corner of the yard, chewing some straw and shaking his head.

The engine tone changed once more. It sounded like it was slowing down.

This time, when it emerged from behind the barn, it was flying slowly enough for Charlie and Rhodri to recognize the machine. It was a gyrocopter.

Auntie had rejoined the children in the yard and still had the walkie-talkie switched on.

'All stations, Sparrow One, final to land runway one-zero at Drakepuddle.'

Charlie stared as the machine made a gentle turn and an arrester hook emerged from the underside. The aircraft made a few very minor corrections to its flight path then disappeared behind the side of the farmhouse.

The children started running to follow it as it vanished behind the corner of a wall.

Before they had taken more than a few strides, they heard a faint squeak of tyres, followed very shortly afterwards, by the noise of an engine accelerating to full speed briefly and then slowing, almost immediately, to an idle.

By the time they reached the corner of the house, the engine had become all but silent. The flying machine must have landed, but where?

Charlie had seen a few strange things at Drakepuddle Farm, but what he saw next made him gasp.

'Whoa!' he said as he skidded to a halt. He blinked, wondering if he was seeing things.

Parked a little distance away from the wall of the farmhouse was an immaculate-looking double-decker bus. He read the words in the rear panel.

10. SORRY NOT IN SERVICE

It wasn't the bus that surprised him — he'd seen it dozens of times before —it was what was on the roof that astonished him. Perched on the very top, Uncle had undone his harness and was getting out of the stationary gyrocopter, unstrapping his helmet. Doris, also wearing a crash helmet, was barking excitedly in the rear seat.

22

The Hunter was not in any mood to mess about with niceties. He hated ladders and had been up at four in the morning to climb one, and he cared for early mornings even less than he cared for ladders. But for the next five or ten minutes, none of that would have to matter.

Jasper Allsop's family were just sitting down for lunch when the doorbell rang.

'I'm so sorry to trouble you,' the Hunter spoke softly, as though his disguise wasn't only making him look weak and frail, but actually feeling that way too. 'I've lost my pet budgerigar, and I wonder if you might have seen him? He flew off and I think I saw him coming in this direction, but my old eyes … well, I'm afraid they're not quite what they used to be.'

'I ain't seen him. Hang on. I'll ask my lad,' Mr Allsop

said. 'Oi! Jasper. There's a bloke here who's lost a budgie. You ain't seen it in the garden, have you?'

Allsop came to the door. He took a quick look at the old man's strange face and watery eyes. He looked down to the man's walking frame and snorted.

'He's such a dear little creature. His name's Percy. He has quite the most wonderful plumage, bright turquoise, the friendliest little white face you could imagine and—'

'No. Ain't seen him.'

'Oh, well, thank you for your time. Do you think I may leave this card? I'm offering a reward to anyone who finds him. I don't have much money, but he's such a wonderful companion. He's priceless to me.'

'A reward? How much?' Allsop and his father said together.

23

Everyone spent lunchtime talking about the gyrocopter and how thrilling it must be to land it on the roof of a double-decker bus.

'Nothin' new about landin' aircraft on boats. It's easy after a bit of practice. In fact, I used me Tradget to calculate the crosswind,' Uncle said.

'*Boats?* But what about *buses*?' Rhodri asked.

'Buses, boats: much the same! She's called Jenny, by the way, and landing ain't the hard part. She's got to have rocket-assisted take-off packs to get her airborne, unless I put a catapult on the roof, but I don't want to spoil the deck,' Uncle replied, chuckling and taking a bite from his sandwich.

'You must be bloomin' brave to land it on a tiny deck like that. Just as well it *wasn't* foggy,' Rhodri said.

'*Foggy?* What are you on about? It's as clear as a bottle of Auntie's gin out there.'

'Oh, an alarm went off on my bike on the way here, predicting fog–. I was going to tell you. I wondered if it might be a bug,' Charlie said.' I didn't think it would be, but—'

'Nonsense! Give it here. There ain't no bugs in that computer.'

Charlie handed his bike computer to Uncle who connected it up to a sleek-looking device on the table using a cable he'd whipped out of his pocket. The screen flickered to life.

'The Tradget'll tell us if there's a bug or not. Fog? In the middle of a clear summer day? I've heard it all now.'

'Jenny?' asked Charlie. 'Who's called Jenny...? And what's a *Tradget?*'

'Jenny the gyrocopter. Who else did you think I was talkin' about? Oh – and a Tradget is a *trajectory gadget* – controls all sorts of stuff - gyrocopters, planes, boats, bikes, buses... all sorts. I'll soon check the settings on your bike computer with this.' Uncle fiddled with the device for a few seconds. 'Well, I never. It *did* predict fog. Must've been some kind of localized phenomenon. Bloomin' odd!'

No one spoke for a few moments. Everyone watched Uncle scratching his head. Suddenly, his expression changed and he dropped the Tradget on the table.

'But still, you must be brave, landing on a tiny deck like that,' Rhodri said.

Uncle unclipped the cable from the Tradget and slid Charlie's bike computer back across the table and got up from his chair.

'I put three arrester wires on that deck,' he said. 'What's to be afraid of? If it weren't safe, do you think I'd take Doris up with me?' He looked at Rhodri over the top of his spectacles. 'Being brave ain't nothin' to do with being afraid or not. I've been lucky enough to know some right brave fellas: soldiers rescuin' folk from all sorts of terrible, ghastly places; puttin' the well-being of total strangers in front of their own safety. But if you ask 'em if they were scared, they'll tell you they was as scared as a mouse pinchin' the cream at a tomcat's tea party. Being brave don't mean you ain't scared about what you're doin'; being brave is about being scared and still doin' it!'

'Oh. Sorry,' Rhodri said. Although it seemed obvious that he wasn't really sure what he was apologizing for.

'Er, your Tradget looks a bit like a tablet. Do you have any games on it?' Charlie asked, trying to lighten the mood.

'It *was* a tablet once. In fact, it were about a dozen of 'em but the old-fashioned innards weren't up to much, so I tuned it up a bit, and no, I ain't got any games on it.'

'So, what do you have on it? Ministry stuff?'

Uncle grabbed the Tradget and left the room without saying a word.

*

After lunch, Poppy and Bryony took Doris for a quick run over the fields with Uncle. Charlie found himself alone with Auntie whilst Rhodri went to get something from his rucksack.

'Have you ever had a go at flying Jenny?' Charlie asked.

'Not yet! I've flown a few aeroplanes over the years. We used to use one for crop-spraying. Can't do that anymore though.'

'Why not?'

'Rules and regulations! Shame though. I used to enjoy that. We've still got it in one of the barns, I often hear your uncle tinkering around with it.'

'Auntie Chloe?' Charlie asked.

'I know that tone,' she replied, 'Your curiosity getting the better of you again?'

'What was up with Uncle Pip earlier? He seemed kind of angry about something.'

'Oh, he's probably just a bit annoyed that there's a bug in your bike computer. He's a bit of a perfectionist.'

'But he said it wasn't a bug. It's nothing to do with the Minatauri or any of that, is it?'

Charlie could tell from Auntie's expression that he was dangerously close to being told where his curiosity was and wasn't welcome.

'He told me they killed his parents. He said they made him … *the way he is*. What happened?'

Auntie took a deep breath.

'Sorry, I shouldn't have asked,' Charlie said.

'Well, I suppose you might as well hear it from me as anyone else. Just don't let on I told you.' Auntie slid her chair closer to Charlie. 'It happened when he was young, about seven years old. His parents were taking him to school when an armed mob appeared out of nowhere, some kind of private army. They started shooting and your uncle's parents were hit. We'll never know if it was an accident or not, but they were both killed. He's convinced it was the Minatauri. Your uncle escaped. He ran off and hid in an underground drain for a few days. That's why he's petrified of going into tunnels or drains, and it's why he hates rats.'

'But who's Flack, and why does he think he had something to do with it?'

'Flack was there. He saw what happened. Apparently he was nearly killed too. He would only have been about eighteen at the time himself. Later, Flack got a job at the Ministry, and your Uncle Pip recognized him. He had something about him that was ... unusual, distinctive. He had—'

'He had what?'

Auntie had stopped talking. She smiled over Charlie's shoulder. 'Oh hi, Rhodri. I didn't see you come in,' she said, picking up a single dirty teaspoon which she put it in a small jar on the kitchen worktop next to the sink. Four long, shiny metal arms emerged from beneath the wall cupboards. They looked like human arms, only with way too many elbow joints. They picked up the dirty dishes and cutlery from the kitchen table with their white-gloved hands, cleaned and dried the dishes, then began sorting them into order and putting them away into their respective cupboards, all in perfect coordination with each other, as well as the other objects in the room, including

Poppy and Bryony who had just returned with Doris. Charlie laughed as Bryony tried to dodge the plates and pans, which whizzed within inches of her head.

'You don't need to duck, Bryony. It actually slows them down!' Charlie said.

'Wow! It does the washing-up. That's ace!' Bryony said. 'My mum would love one of those. She *hates* cleaning dishes and plates.'

The entire clean-up was completed in less time than it took Auntie to fold up her tea towels and hang them neatly on the handrail in front of the kitchen stove.

'What was all that about earlier?' Rhodri asked Charlie. 'Your uncle seemed really cross about something.'

'Oh probably nothing,' Charlie replied.

'Charlie's uncle saw some things in his military days; things he doesn't like to talk about. Best not mention it really. Now then, who likes chocolate meltdown megaton truffles? I'm making a bucket load for tea, but first I need to straighten the crankshaft on the number three tractor and fix the roof on Nosebag's stable,' Auntie added.

*

'I can't believe that the cars drive around by themselves,' Rhodri said, fiddling with the model railway in their bedroom, 'and it's brilliant the way it just turns upside-down into a bed when you push that small telephone box down. What else does your uncle have?'

'You haven't seen the loft room yet, have you? You've got to see that!' Charlie said.

'Why? What's in there? Any of his secret army stuff?'

'There's all sorts of cool stuff in there. Come on, I'll

show you. Maybe we *can* find some of his old army things.'

The two boys burst out of their room onto the landing and almost knocked Poppy flying. She was carrying a handful of magazines for her and Bryony.

'Hey, watch it, losers!' she said. 'You almost made me drop these over the banister.'

Inside the room, stacked from floor to ceiling, there were boxes and boxes of books. On each of the wooden boxes, the contents were described: *PHYSICS; CHEMISTRY; BIOLOGY; GEOGRAPHY; MODERN HISTORY; MILITARY HISTORY; REFERENCE; POETRY; FICTION A–E; FICTION F–K; FICTION L–P; FICTION Q–Z.* There were several other classifications too. There must have been at least 100 identical boxes, all neatly stacked.

Charlie noticed the bewildered expression on Rhodri's face.

'He moved everything out of the loft into here when he built his Ideas Room upstairs,' he explained. 'He never got round to moving the bedroom furniture out first though.'

'Probably came in handy for a rest, judging by the amount of stuff he had to move! And it all seems so well organized,' Rhodri said. 'Did your uncle do that?'

'No! My Aunt Chloe did all the labelling; she likes everything to be in its proper place. Uncle Pip says she gets it from sorting out her record collection. Look over here, it's my uncle's first train set, and it's still in the original box,' Charlie said. 'He set it up last Christmas. It was awesome. He made some extra track and had it driving round the kitchen with mince pies and chocolates in the wagons. Come on, let's look for some old army gear.'

'Look!' said Rhodri. 'That looks a bit creepy. What is it?' he asked, pointing to a strange mask hanging from a nail in the wall.

'It's an old gas mask. I think that *is* from his army days.'

'Can I try it on?' asked Rhodri.

'Okay, I'll see if I can find the helmet and the rest of his uniform.'

Rhodri took the gas mask from the wall and placed it over his face. Almost immediately he removed it.

'It smells weird,' he said, 'really rubbery.'

'Give it here. I'll have a go.' Charlie placed the mask over his face and sipped in half a breath of rubbery air. 'I see what you mean,' he said in a muffled splutter.

'You look and sound like an alien!'

'Hey! We could sneak in on Poppy and Bryony tonight and give them the fright of their lives with this!' He took off the mask and placed it on the floor. 'I bet his uniform is under here,' he said, removing a sheet, which covered a rail of old clothes.

'It is, look!'

'What did he do in the army anyway? Did he join up so he could fight the Minatauri? After they killed his ...' Rhodri realized that, maybe he should have kept his mouth shut, 'parents?' he finished in a low voice.

'What? You heard my Auntie talking about that? She wasn't even supposed to tell me! And now Rhodri Motor-Mouth knows all about it. You'd better not tell anyone.'

'Sorry. There's no need to be like that.' Rhodri said.

'Have you ever tried it on? The uniform?' he added, try-ing to change the subject.

'Don't be daft. It would be miles too big!'

'Why don't you give it a go?'

Charlie carefully removed the green jacket from the hanger and slipped it on over his t-shirt. It hung loosely. When he swung his arms, the sleeves were so long that they brushed the floor.

'You look like an ape, with your arms dangling down like that! Try the trousers on,' said Rhodri.

Charlie removed the trousers from the rail. As he did so, something fell from one of the pockets and landed on the floor with a dull thud.

'What's that?' he said.

He picked up a tangled, crimson ribbon, which un-wound rapidly. The object at the end of the ribbon swung heavily in front of Charlie's knees: a dark, bronze medal in the shape of a cross. He held it up for a closer look. Attached to the cross was a bar. He studied the words engraved on it: *487239 SGT P CLUNCKLE 264 SIGNALS SQUADRON*

He glanced at the centre of the cross. In the middle of the circle, there was a date, which looked like it had been scratched out.

Charlie flicked the medal over in his hand.

There was relief of some sort raised above the cross: a lion perched on top of a crown.

He read the inscription embossed on the front of the cross.

'*For Valour?*'

24

Charlie woke trying to kick his legs free, which were tangled in his sheets. He was sweating.

'What? Where am I? What am I doing in the playground in my pyjamas?' He flopped one leg out over the edge of his bed. 'Oh, I'm in …' he started to say, but a yawn interrupted him. He could see that Rhodri was talking but couldn't hear what he was saying. He sat up and rubbed his eyes.

'I said, are you okay? You look like you've been through a car wash!' Rhodri said. 'I've been awake for ages.'

'I had a weird dream. There was this awful wailing bagpipe music. I woke up at Allsop's house and the phone was ringing.'

'That wasn't wailing bagpipes. It's Poppy's music,' Rhodri said. 'It started ages ago, and your auntie's just rung the bell for breakfast. Can't you smell it cooking?'

*

A large cooked breakfast of eggs, bacon and toast was waiting for them. As soon as Auntie finished serving it up, she started fussing around, packing food and drink into some cool boxes.

'Can't have you going hungry,' she said.

'Where's Uncle?' Poppy asked.

'He's been up since dawn, tinkering,' replied Auntie.

'Talkin' about me, are you? Me ears may be failin' me, but me nose is workin' alright!' Uncle said, walking into the kitchen and wiping his hands on an old rag, which he discarded onto the back of a chair. 'I reckon everythin's tickety-boo on the Number Ten. Just made some final adjustments. We set off at eight o'clock!'

'Why so early?' asked Charlie, 'It only takes an hour to drive to Ottlebridge'.

'Yep, but we're going the *pretty* way, and we ain't necessarily *only* goin' to Ottlebridge. Maybe we're goin' somewhere else afterwards! After breakfast and teeth-brushin', I want you all to pack them rucksacks and suitcases with enough clothes for three days.'

'An overnight stay? Bring our pyjamas? Yay! That's amazing!' said Bryony, who had politely finished chewing her food before speaking.

'Woo hoo! An adventure!' added Rhodri, who hadn't.

'*Three days?* Pack enough for three days in less than *one hour?*' protested Poppy.

'Oh, it's not that bad. I'll help you,' Auntie said. 'Just five more mouths to feed, then I'm all yours.' She'd just finished packing up the cool boxes and picked up a mixing bowl and took it towards the large dresser and opened the door. Inside there was a refrigerator mounted on the wall, next to a small oven. Several pipes led neatly down and emerged into five machines on the floor, which looked like old-fashioned food blenders. Underneath every machine there was a bowl, each bearing the name of one of auntie's cats: *MOGG*; *MORGAN*; *MORRIS*; *MINNIE*; and *MYOOO*. 'There's plenty of mice to catch, but you can't beat a bit of home cooking! I do wish Morgan wasn't such a fussy eater though!' she said.

Charlie stood up and ran towards the stairs, shouting something that nobody could understand because he had a mouthful of bacon sandwich.

25

'Oh you've found my Percy! How wonderful,' the Hunter said, standing up and collecting a large sack and the keys to an unmarked white van. 'Up a tree near your house? No, he doesn't move much, he's very shy. Straight away if possible, in case he does fly away. Can I meet you there? Yes, of course I'll bring the reward. Oh, I'm not sure I could climb a ladder. You'll do it for an extra ten pounds you say? Well, I suppose I could go without my fish and chip supper for a week or two.'

26

Eventually even Poppy had given in to the infectious excitement. Somehow, Auntie had talked her into leaving most of her home comforts behind too. She'd stubbornly insisted on bringing her own music though: there had been no way she was getting on a bus which only had a wind-up clockwork radio.

When everyone finally got to the door with their bags, the bus was waiting for them. A bike rack had been fixed to the rear. Somehow, Uncle had managed to get all the bikes attached to the upper deck. The gyrocopter was tethered firmly to the roof too, with its rotors fixed in place by some cables.

Uncle was sitting in the driver's seat with his door open. He appeared to be reading something and checking gauges on the bus's instrument panel. Every so often, he'd look at the panel or flick a switch, then return to whatever he was reading.

'All aboard!' he shouted when he saw Charlie and Rhodri. 'One adult, four children and a dog. Return to Myst'ryville!' He pressed a button and a small bell chimed six times. '£10.43, please!'

'Bagsy the front row upstairs!' Rhodri called as he ran, dragging his rucksack along the dusty yard towards the chugging vehicle.

'Bagsy that all you like!' replied Charlie. 'But I'm bagsying the seat right behind the driver.'

As Charlie approached the bus, he saw the sun glinting off the shiny wheel trims. He'd never noticed it before, but they had overlapping capital letter Rs embossed in them and the rims were painted in exactly the same gleaming colour as the rest of the bus. *So that was why the car in the red barn was on bricks*, he thought.

Rhodri ran up the stairs to the top deck and flung his rucksack onto the first seat he could find. As he turned to get to the front row, he stopped dead.

There was no front row!

Or second row.

And probably no third row either.

Instead, there was a large gap where the first few rows of seats would normally be. It was like he was standing on a balcony inside the bus, overlooking the driver's position.

Charlie ran up the stairs. 'What do you reckon to that?' he asked.

Rhodri turned around. Behind a couple of rows of ordinary seats, there was a large polished, wooden table and, either side of that two comfortable looking sofas. There were also some rather smart chests of drawers and a selection of furniture that wouldn't have looked out of place inside a very plush hotel.

Rhodri looked at the floor. He was standing on an extremely expensive-looking carpet. Eventually, he stopped gaping around the inside of the bus.

'It's er ...' he started.

'I know. Bet you've never been on a bus like this before,' Charlie said.

'Er, it's ... um ...'

'Cool? Awesome?' Charlie suggested.

'*Weird!*' Rhodri finally said.

'Wicked, isn't it!' Charlie replied.

Poppy, Bryony and Auntie boarded the bus via the platform at the back and placed their cases next to a wardrobe. There would be plenty of time to unpack later.

Uncle revved the engine and the bus began to move off down the long, dusty driveway leading to Great Disbury. Everyone was so busy waving and shouting goodbye to Nosebag, no one heard the telephone inside the farmhouse ring.

27

'Where do you reckon we're going?' Rhodri asked.

'I don't know,' Charlie replied. 'It's a mystery, like he said. All I know is we're going the pretty way, whatever that is.'

The bus splashed through the ford and over the narrow railway bridge, heading towards the village green. When it stopped at the junction opposite the Pig and Whistle, Charlie noticed Uncle was looking at a strange display projected onto the windscreen. It seemed to be a copy of the Tradget screen, which had been attached to a flexible mount on the dashboard and appeared to show all of the vehicles, pedestrians and other nearby hazards. It even showed a black cat crossing the road a few hundred metres away. Charlie shuffled in his seat so he was directly behind his uncle and had the same driver's-eye view of the windscreen.

There was a list of words projected in line with the various houses and cottages. Some of the words were green and some were red. *BAKER ... DELTA ... TANGO ... VICTOR*

As the bus approached the Post Office, he noticed the word *GEORGE* projected on the windscreen in line with the building. Strangely, as the bus got closer, Godfrey Blessings stepped outside with his watering can and lifted his hand to acknowledge Uncle. Next to the word *GEORGE*, some more writing had appeared:

> *STATUS: RESIDENT ... GREEN*
> *MEMO: BURTHDAY 5 DAZE ...*
> *LIKES: CARS, ENJINS, GARDNIN*
> *DISLIKES: CABBIJ, TOMARTO SOOP,*
> *FLIP-FLOPS, SNAYKES AND LADDURS*

Charlie suspected his uncle had added the memo items himself.

George? he thought. But wasn't his name Godfrey?

He looked up to see Uncle's eyes in the rear-view mirror staring directly back at him.

'Nine lives, Charlie. Nine lives,' he whispered.

Uncle didn't pay any attention to the cyclist who had stopped for a rest on the bench opposite the Post Office. The man was holding a metal flask. He undid the lid and lifted it towards his lips, as if to take a drink.

Charlie saw him though, and he noticed some words which had appeared next to him on the side of the windscreen:

> *NON-RESIDENT. TRANSMITTING DEVICE*
> *DETECTED.*

As he watched the cyclist, Charlie saw him do something strange.

He started talking ... into his flask.

28

'Beautiful day to be ridin' in a double-decker bus through these country roads, ain't it?' Uncle said.

The rising sun had burnt away all of the early morning mist and he started whistling to himself as he guided the bus along the narrow, winding lanes.

'Perfect!' replied Charlie. 'Where are we going?'

'Oh, don't worry about that. I'll take care of the navigatin'. You just enjoy the scenery.'

Rhodri nudged the rucksack out of the way and slid into the seat next to Charlie.

'Actually, this *is* the coolest bus I've ever been on,' he said.

'It's my uncle's pride and joy,' replied Charlie. 'He's been working on it for ages. You should have seen it when he first bought it. It was a right mess.'

'It were barely a runner!' interrupted Uncle. 'Had to have new pistons; total rebuild of the cylinder head; fuel pulse instantators needed dechunterin'; propshaft weren't straight; no superchargin' to speak of; no auxiliary power whatsoever; alternator like summat off a Model T Ford; leaks all over the place. You would not believe the leaks! No navigation system; no multi-state propulsion means. In fact, I'm still working on that ... what you might call a bit of a project!'

'Oh,' replied Rhodri, not really understanding any-thing. 'It's a shame you got rid of the front seats upstairs though. I always love sitting at the front of the top deck.'

'Me too. Got your seat belt on?'

'Er, no,' replied Rhodri.

'Buckle up then. And, Charlie, put that bag on your lap.'

Rhodri fastened his seat belt and passed the rucksack to Charlie. As he placed his rucksack on his knee, a small light on the dashboard changed from red to green. Uncle moved a lever upwards and a two-tone chime, very much like a doorbell, began sounding. The driver's seat and the first two rows of passengers' seats began to lift upwards, guided by shiny metal poles on each side of the bus's in-terior.

'What's happening?' Rhodri asked.

'Comes in handy if you're stuck in traffic jams this!' Uncle replied. 'You can see what's causin' it!'

The chiming continued as the seats rose further up-wards.

'How fast are we driving?' Charlie asked.

'About fifty,' Uncle replied.

'It's just like we're taking off in an old aeroplane.' Charlie looked out over the hedges as the seats rose higher. Uncle was still guiding the bus expertly around the sweeping lanes with the large steering wheel.

'Wow! This is AWESOME!' said Rhodri.

'You can see the windmill at Quillton from here!' Charlie said, pointing out of the window to a white-capped windmill in the far distance.

'And if you look over there, you can see the mast on

Signal Hill. That's got to be fifteen miles from here! We're just comin' up to Flatt Bottom,' Uncle said. 'You should get a good view of the airfield as we come round this next corner. You won't have seen it in your dad's car 'cause the hedges is too high.'

They were still craning their necks as they drove past the Ruddy Duck pub and the flowery sign reminding visitors to drive carefully.

Charlie was enjoying the views over the walls into the back gardens beyond, when an orange warning started blinking on a box at the edge of the dashboard.

'What does that mean?' he asked. 'Is everything okay?'

'That's a communication alarm.'

A small strip of paper printed out from the ticket machine, which Uncle ripped off and read. At the same time, some more text appeared on the windscreen:

COMMUNICATION SYSTEM:
MISSED TELEPHONE CALL FROM CRUMP
HOUSEOLD
REPLAY MESSAGE?

The bus came to a halt, at the side of the road, and Uncle applied the handbrake.

'Looks like your mum and dad tried to phone. Better see what they want.'

'I can't believe you can do all this from the top of a bus!' Rhodri said.

Everyone listened to the recording of Mrs Crump's voice.

When the message stopped, there was a moment of silence.

'Allsop's gone missing?' said Charlie, looking at Rhodri. 'Why?'

29

'How do they know he's missing?' Rhodri asked.

'He said he was going to help an old man get a budgie down from a tree, and never came back; just disappeared,' Auntie said. 'His parents wondered if you'd seen him.'

'Why would anyone take Allsop?' Charlie asked.

'They haven't said he's been taken. They're only worried about where he is. He could have run off. Maybe he's embarrassed about what happened at school, maybe he's ashamed?' Poppy suggested, turning towards Charlie.

Charlie fidgeted in his seat.

'Allsop, embarrassed? Ashamed? He's not the type to run away,' Bryony added.

'Probably gone off somewhere with those two drongo friends of his,' Rhodri interrupted.

'Your mum said someone saw a white van driving away in a hurry, that's why they're worried. There was a ladder propped up near a tree not far from his house. Anyway, he doesn't sound the type to run off to me,' Auntie said. 'What do you think?' she added, turning to Uncle.

'Probably nothin' to worry about. He'll turn up sooner or later, and it ain't nothin' to do with what he pinched off Charlie. I don't reckon the side effects will have lasted *this* long.'

'It's probably just some stupid game, just like I was trying to say,' Bryony added. 'Let's not worry too much just 'cause Allsop's gone astray.'

'But what if he's been kidnapped or something *because* of what happened? What if somebody wants to find out why he behaved so strangely?' Charlie said.

'I'm sure he'll turn up. What can we do anyway? Come on, are we goin' to have some fun or what?' Uncle pressed a button and the engine chugged back to life.

Just as they were about to move off, another light started flashing; this time a red one.

'Now what?' Uncle tore off another strip of paper from the ticket machine and Charlie read the words projected onto the windscreen:

> *SECURITY SYSTEM*
> *TRESPASS ALERT: DRAKEPUDDLE FARM*
> *DISPLAY CAMERAS?*

Almost immediately afterwards, the name *GEORGE* started blinking on the screen too, shorty followed by *VICTOR* and *BAKER*.

'Better 'ave a look. At least I know it won't be one of your auntie's cats. I finally managed to get 'em all to wear their locata-collars. Morgan was havin' none of it at first'.

A dozen or so images projected themselves onto the

large windscreen, all views from the various security cameras at Drakepuddle Farm.

After a second or so, Charlie spotted something through one of the cameras.

'Look! Who are those three men standing near the back door?'

He pointed at the image on the windscreen. 'There! Who are they?'

'That's odd. They don't look they're up to much good. I hope they ain't tryin' to break in 'cause they're in for some nasty surprises if they are. What's puzzlin' me is that they don't seem to have a vehicle. If they're burglars, how do they plan to get away with any loot?'

He tapped on the Tradget screen a couple of times and a small joystick emerged from the left-hand side of the dashboard.

A set of flashing green crosshairs appeared.

'It looks like he's walking backwards towards that basket.' Poppy said.

'I'm just rewindin' it. There! That's how they got in.'

'A hot-air balloon!' Rhodri said.

They watched as the balloon inflated before them, seemingly without need for a gas burner and took off. It floated away until it was a tiny dot, visible in just one of the screens.

'Who would come to burgle your house in a hot-air balloon?' Charlie asked. 'Surely it would be about the worst way of getting to the right place to start with, let alone being able to make a quick getaway.' he added.

'Even if they did break in, they'd never get away quickly enough. A policeman on a bike would probably be able to keep up with a balloon. It just doesn't make any sense,' Poppy said.

'Should we phone the police?' Charlie suggested.

'They might just be balloonists, knocking on the door to use the telephone. You know, to arrange to be picked up,' Rhodri said.

'They weren't askin' to use no phone. Whoever it was had a walkie-talkie. You could see 'em talking into it. And that weren't no ordinary balloon. It had thruster jets to control its flight path. It landing at Drakepuddle was no accident. Look, the blighters *are* tryin' to get in.'

He was right. The three figures were busy cutting through wires and cables.

Uncle was staring at the screen. He seemed to mutter something to himself under his breath. It wasn't very loud, but it sounded like a single, whispered word: '*Minatauri.*'

'They're tryin' to isolate the power and telephone lines. I don't like the look of this. I'm phonin' your mum and dad, Charlie. I want to get 'em up to Drakepuddle. I want 'em out of danger.'

'*OUT* of danger?' Poppy asked. 'Won't you be sending them right into the middle of it? What if those men are armed? What if they—?'

'Yeah, I think you should phone the police, Uncle.' Charlie said.

'I think I know what's goin' on here. Them arriving in that balloon is the perfect way to seem innocent. Balloons are always landin' in fields round Drakepuddle. Nowt suspicious about that and, like you said, Charlie, how could they possibly make a quick getaway? They'll have thought of that. As for your mum and dad,' he said, turning to Poppy, 'I can get 'em into that house safely without bein' noticed and you have to believe me, there is *nowhere safer.*' He turned to face the windscreen again. When he spoke, it was in a tone Charlie hadn't heard before. 'If I need to get 'em out of there, I can get 'em out fast, *real fast.*

30

Allsop hated his cell. There was no window. An awful fluorescent strip light flickered behind a stained panel in the ceiling, and there was no way of switching it off. He couldn't even tell if it was night or day, unless he turned the TV on, and he didn't want to do that. Not anymore.

His captor had taken the blindfold off as soon as he was inside his cell.

If only he hadn't.

Not that it had been very effective anyway. It was tied so tightly that it had left a gap between his nose and his cheeks. He'd been able to see clearly, albeit only downward, towards his feet. But he'd soon discovered that, by tilting his head back, he could see forwards too. That's what he had done whilst he was locked in the back of the van, tracing its tracks, looking out of the small rear window until his neck was stiff. He'd recognized much of the scenery. He'd been able to read the names of the villages he had been driven through. He'd even seen the writing on the gates leading to this awful place. The man had stopped to close them after turning into the yard. They'd swung all the way open, revealing the location to Jasper Allsop in rusty, six-inch-high writing. He knew exactly where he was … at least he had, until everything had gone dark.

If only it had stayed dark.

The next time he saw light, he was being led down a corridor. He noticed, through the small slit of a window he had into his new world, that there were other people there too. He'd seen their feet. Something about them seemed strange. Certainly not the sort of behaviour he'd expected to see inside a dark cellar or underground cavern. The feet were moving, shuffling in time with some music; music that was playing constantly through-out the building or tunnel, or whatever this dank, noisy place was.

When the man took the blindfold off, Allsop almost begged for him to put it back on.

When he had first lay down on the dirty, damp mattress, that face just wouldn't go away. He tried to sleep. It was no good; the man had the kind of face that wasn't possible to forget and it was there whenever Allsop closed his eyes.

At first, the television had provided a bit of a distraction, even a thrill. He saw his own photo and name appear on the screen. The thrill soon faded when he saw his parents upset and pleading for him to come home.

The more he learnt about his disappearance, the more obvious it became that no one had any idea who had taken him, or where he was. He was sure that he'd be stuck here, in this flickering cell, in this weird underground prison listening to that strange music forever.

He hadn't eaten. He wasn't hungry. He felt like his stomach was full of gravel and there was a big lump of it stuck at the back of his throat.

Some keys jangled and he heard the cough he recognized. The man was back.

The door unlocked and his captor stepped inside.

His skin looked tight, like a mask that was too small for his face, and his oily complexion meant that his glasses keep sliding down his nose. He was constantly pushing them back into place. Through them, Allsop recognized those watery eyes.

The man was carrying a notepad and a pen, which he put on a crate in the corner of the room. He walked as if he hated having to waste his energy moving his arms and legs. And when he talked, he didn't look at Jasper, but spoke to the floor a few feet in front of himself, in a whiny, gurgling voice. He didn't care much for talking.

'I need you to write a little note. You have to say you're okay. Everyone's going to want to know you're still … alive.'

'*Okay?* I am *not* okay! How can I possibly be okay, you weirdo? Stuck down here, listening to that damn music the whole time. I could not be *less* okay.'

'Just write a note, say that you *are* okay, or I'll take the TV away,' the man said.

The man coughed again and walked out of the room, the music getting briefly louder as he opened the door. The jangling of the keys confirmed that it was locked.

Jasper got up off the mattress to pick up the notepad

and pen. He looked at the thick block of paper. There was not one, but two slim notepads: a blank one for him to write on and another pad too, which he flicked through. It was full of drawings and sketches. He began slowly thumbing through the pages.

Almost straight away, he heard the keys rattling against the thick door.

Hurriedly he put both notepads and the pen back in exactly the same place he'd found them.

He'd only just got back to his mattress, when the door opened once more. The man and his music burst back into the room.

For the first time, the man looked Allsop in the eye. Instinctively, Allsop looked away.

'You haven't started writing your note yet, have you?'

'No. I'm just going to do it now.'

'Good.' The man's brow wrinkled into an expression quite unlike any that Jasper had seen before. 'So you haven't … picked up the notepad then?'

'No.'

Without taking his eyes away from Jasper, the man picked up the second notepad from underneath the blank one, then left the room and locked the door.

'Wait. Who are you?' Allsop said.

The man turned around and smiled. It was a cold smile. Only the narrowest of gaps opened up between his lips. His eyes flickered.

'I am the Hunter,' he said.

31

Charlie watched as the intruders cut through the electricity cable with a chainsaw.

'Aren't you worried about the damage?' he asked.

'Got me own electric generators at Drakepuddle. I could keep most of the county lit up if I wanted to! Those 'uns they're cuttin' through are used mainly for doin' me Christmas lights.'

'They're going to try and break in with a crowbar,' Rhodri said. 'Look, they're trying to wedge the kitchen door open with it.'

Uncle shook his head. 'Put the kettle on, will you? This is going to be worth watching.'

They watched as the intruders tried to force open the kitchen door with the large metal bar. It wouldn't give way, almost as if the door was made of solid steel and welded shut. Even the full weight of all three men didn't cause the door to budge.

'They'll never get in with that! The locking mechanism on them doors goes a foot into the bricks, and every one of them bricks and the lock itself is made out of Hyperstrontanium. Even the whitewash is bulletproof,' Uncle said.

Charlie remembered the bricks which had been propping up the old car in the Red Barn. There had been five or six spare ones in a neat pile. He'd knocked them over by accident once and had been surprised how light they had been when he picked them up. 'But they look like normal bricks. I don't understand,' he said. 'Why are they so strong?'

'Strong stuff Hyperstrontanium! I borrowed one of your auntie's hatboxes once to make a mould with it. I filled it with molten Hyperstrontanium and when it set, I had the strongest hatbox in the world! The people in the bank couldn't believe it when I filled it with dynamite and sat on the lid. They thought I were mad.'

'What? You sat on a box full of dynamite … in a bank?' Rhodri's mouth didn't close at the end of the sentence. 'Don't tell me you lit it.'

'Course! How else were I supposed to show 'em how strong it was?'

'What happened?' Poppy asked.

'They ran away!'

'No, I meant, what happened to you?'

'Oh, it were a bit like trouser-trumpetin' on an old tin trunk: just a tiny rumble and it were all over. The banks all use Hyperstrontanium safes now, to keep their valuables in. Those bricks have a veneer on 'em so they look like normal house bricks, and a special whitewash.' Uncle patted his pocket and looked at Charlie. 'Bet you two quid they try and break a window next.'

'I think you might be right.' said Bryony, pointing towards one of the screens.

'Look, one of them has a hammer … or an axe,' Charlie said.

'And he's swinging it with all his might!' Bryony

added.

'That's goin' to hurt him much more than the window.'

The man hit the hammer hard against the glass but it stopped dead on impact. The intruder dropped the hammer and started shaking his hand, obviously in considerable pain.

'That glass is all an inch thick and octo-glazed. It's got Hyperstrontanium fibres in it too. You can only break it from the inside.'

'Aren't you going to do anything to stop them?' Poppy asked.

'And why won't you call the police?' Charlie added.

'All that can be done has been done. Anyhow, they'll get fed up of tryin' sooner or later and go home, I expect. Let's listen in, shall we?'

Uncle flicked a few switches on a panel over his head and the sounds of the commotion outside the farmhouse played out through some speakers somewhere inside the bus.

One of the figures had returned from the balloon basket with a large, rectangular box, which he placed on the floor some distance from the wall of the farmhouse. He unlatched the lid and removed something and pointed it towards the window. The unmistakeable noise of machine-gun fire echoed throughout the bus.

Uncle zoomed in. The bullets had all landed with a dull thud before turning into dozens of deformed blobs, which slid down the window like small, black slugs.

The intruder took aim again and emptied an entire magazine of bullets into the window and surrounding brickwork. The bullets dribbled to the floor as before.

'Cheeky blighters!' said Uncle. 'I'll have to wipe the bullet marks off the whitewash now.'

Auntie leant forward to pass Charlie's uncle a cup of coffee. She shook her head. 'Oh, where did they learn to shoot? A duck-shooting gallery at the fairground?' she tutted. 'What an utter disgrace! See, even Nosebag is shaking his head.'

Uncle reached down and pressed a button on the dash-board:

'OI! I 'OPE YOU'RE GOIN' TO PAY FOR THAT!'

The three figures glanced around, searching for the source of the voice. One of them picked up his walkie-talkie and spoke into it.

'What's he saying?' asked Charlie.

'He knows they've been busted. I'll turn the volume up.'

Charlie watched the man place the walkie-talkie back into his belt clip and signalled to one of his colleagues, who returned with something that was obviously much, much heavier than the machine gun. He staggered, strug-gling with the weight of the object. Instead of walking towards the farmhouse though, he walked in the opposite direction.

'What's he doing now? Why's he walking away?' Rhodri asked.

'Looks like they've brought a rocket launcher — quite a beefy one too by the look of it — so he'll need to be a fair distance away from the blast,' Uncle replied.

'You don't seem very worried about it!' Poppy added.

'Course I'm worried. That's a dangerous weapon! They might 'urt 'emselves!'

The man, who appeared to be the leader of the group, positioned the tube so that it was aiming towards the farmhouse. One of his colleagues unfolded some metal legs from the underside of the tube to form a mount. The third man placed a small box on the ground and removed a large, plump-looking rocket.

Charlie heard a thud as the rocket slid to the base of the launcher. Nosebag trotted off around the corner, still shaking his head.

'Surely you've got to do something now,' he said.

'I'm goin' to finish me cuppa first,' Uncle replied, taking a slurp from his large, flowery mug.

Charlie looked at Rhodri and shrugged. The two watched as the man lifted the base of the tube and rested it on his shoulder. He took his time and shuffled his body. It looked like he was aiming at the kitchen window.

The man fine-tuned his aim.

DOOMPH!

WHOOSH!

The man almost toppled backwards against the force of the rocket launching. A trail of smoke streamed out behind the missile's wake.

The rocket found its target.

BOOOOM!

A deafening blast filled the bus. Nobody spoke as a huge cloud of dust and smoke exploded from the spot where the rocket hit the farmhouse.

32

As usual, Allsop was the centre of attention. Detective Chief Inspector Yarn looked at the photographs of the other faces stuck on the wall. There were pictures of Charlie and his classmates.

'Where do you start with that lot?' he asked.

'Best we could get at short notice,' the policewoman replied. 'The headmaster was incredibly quick to help, especially as it's the school holidays.'

The inspector was holding a piece of paper; it was the note that had been pinned to the tree next to the abandoned ladder.

He read it aloud:

> *The boy is safe. He will be released when the*
> *following conditions are met:*
> *There was a recent episode at Allsford School.*
> *The boy's behaviour was believed to be the result*
> *of a reaction to a food additive he had consumed. I*
> *want the exact details of that additive.*
> *A sample of the substance and precise details of its*
> *ingredients and manufacturing process must be*
> *delivered to a location of my choosing, details of*
> *which will follow.*
> *This must be done by midday on the first day of*

next month.

To prove the boy is well, I will send a handwritten note from him.

'Let's hope we can solve this one before it's too late,' the inspector said.

'What do you mean "too late"?'

'I mean before the first day of next month. Imagine the school holidays and everyone's too frightened to let their children outside, because there's a kidnapper on the loose. Put everyone we can onto the case.'

'Is there anything else can we do?'

'We can try and speak to his classmates, to try and work out what might have happened to him, we ask for anyone who might have seen this van driving away and we go through the crime scene and every statement with a toothpick.'

'Anything else?'

'We wait … for a note. I've got a very bad feeling about this one.'

33

'But look, they're wrecking your house!' Charlie yelled.

'Amateurs!' Uncle muttered under his breath.

Charlie waited for the dust and debris to clear. As the smoke thinned, he saw what was left of the rocket shell splattered against the glass. It sizzled like a giant, jagged,

metal omelette. Hissing fragments slid down the undam-
aged window.

It was totally silent in the farmyard and the bus, at least
for a moment.

'I ONLY CLEANED THEM WINDOWS YESTER-
DAY. NOW GET LOST BEFORE I POINT A ROCKET
AT *YOU*. AND IT'LL BE A LOT SHARPER THAN
THAT PEA SHOOTER WHAT YOU BROUGHT!'

He turned to the children, 'Bloomin' marvellous, ain't
it? I protect Drakepuddle against World War III and a
bunch of dimwits and dunderheads turn up with a two-
bob box of fireworks. Come on, we're on holiday. Who
wants to go boatin'?'

He pressed the start button and the engine chugged
back to life. As if he had just witnessed nothing more unusual than the postman delivering the mail, he began
whistling to himself as he manoeuvred the bus back onto
the road.

34

It was late morning by the time the bus pulled up next to
the slipway at the side of the river. There was a selection
of small leisure craft moored up at the adjoining boatyard:
mainly cabin cruisers, but there were five or six wooden
rowing boats and some old, neglected fibreglass pedalos.

Uncle turned to Charlie and the other children.

'Here we are then,' he said with a smile, 'There's no

better way of spending a beautiful summer's day than a spot of boatin'. And there's no finer spot to do it than the River Pew!'

'Really? Boating?' Charlie asked. 'After all that's happened, we're going ... *boating?*'

'Don't see why not. Perfect day for it, gettin' away from all that commotion.'

'So, are we going to hire some rowing boats or something whilst someone attacks your house with rockets?' asked Rhodri.

'We're not going on one of those, are we? Because if we are, *I'm* not rowing,' Poppy said with a nod towards the rowing boats, 'and I'm definitely not pedalling *that!*' she added, as her glance fell upon one of the faded pedalo boats.

'No! Don't be daft. We're goin' to use our own boat!'

'But you haven't got a boat, have you?' asked Poppy.

'Yes, I 'ave got me own boat, and you're sittin' in it!'

*

It took about five or ten minutes for Uncle to run through a checklist. Meanwhile, Auntie made sure that any loose plates or dishes were safely stowed.

Charlie and Rhodri had been asked to walk around the outside of the bus to make sure all of the lights were working properly.

'I can't believe this bus!' Rhodri said. 'What else can it do?'

'No idea,' replied Charlie. 'I didn't even know the seats moved up and down! Tell you what though, don't you think it's a bit weird that he doesn't want to call the police?'

'Yeah, and why does he want to send your parents to a place that's just been attacked by an armed gang?'

'I know. He doesn't seem at all bothered by it. Maybe we should ask my auntie about it. We'll try and find out what's going on later, when Uncle's not around. I suppose we'd better check these lights though.'

'He said there should be a red one on the left side and a green one on the right.'

'Don't you mean port and starboard,' corrected Charlie, 'as it's a boat?'

Charlie remembered his uncle's words from the previous day. *Buses ... boats ... much the same.*

'Okay Captain Know-it-all, you take the port side. I'll do the starboard then.'

As he walked past the open driver's window, Charlie could hear the ticket machine typing off another strip of paper. He peered in through the window. Uncle was nowhere to be seen, so he reached across and tried to read what it said. It was a thin ribbon of paper, with a series of tiny dots punched out into it. If it meant anything, Charlie had no idea what, except that, somehow, he knew it had something to do with the Minatauri and, he sensed, something to do with him.

*

'I'll just spin the main gyro up and we'll be off,' Uncle said.

There was a jolt and a high-pitched whirring sound joined that of the chugging engine.

'She were all over the place on her sea trials so I changed the gyro axis and increased the spin speed. Stable as a rock now. Not so important on the river, unless, of course, we go round any corners too fast.' he said, winking at Charlie over the top of his glasses.

As the bus drove slowly down the slipway and into the river, it looked as if it was about to sink. Even though Charlie could see it was floating, it felt very weird.

Within seconds, the bus was sailing smoothly along the river and looked quite majestic, as if it were merely driving through a very big puddle. Charlie glanced through the window. The water seemed to come up to just below the level of the front headlights and, when he turned around, he could see it was leaving a very gentle ripple in its wake.

'Just like being on an old canal boat,' Bryony said. 'My parents hired one for the week once. It was so good: lots of colourful flowerpots, brightly painted metal and wood. There's something *so* nice about being afloat!'

'I bet it were lovely, and less of the "old" if you don't mind,' Uncle replied, gently patting the steering wheel. 'Now, who wants to go out on deck?'

'Out on deck?' Rhodri asked, 'How can there be a deck? There's no room for one.'

'If you all squeeze up to the front couple of rows, we'll get some fresh air!' Uncle said.

Charlie was first into his seat. The chiming doorbell sounded and the seats began lifting smoothly upwards again. This time, they didn't stop when they came level with the upper deck. Instead, a section of the roof slid back, like the sunroof of his dad's car, and the seats continued up through the ceiling. They stopped with a reassuring clunk when they were level with the roof. After a second or two, Charlie recognized the windscreen from the old Rolls Royce in his uncle's barn as it popped up in front of them to act as a windbreak.

'Wow! This is cool' he said.

'I think the nautical term for where we're sittin' is a flyin' bridge! You can undo your seat belts; the deck has a non-slip coating of special grass, but no jumpin' off the side!'

Charlie had never seen the upper surface of the roof before. It was covered in a layer of lush green grass. And around the edge, a perimeter of chrome upright bars had appeared, joined together by a silver chain, presumably to stop anyone falling off the deck. The small staircase also opened up into a neatly railed clearing just behind where Charlie was sitting.

'Shall I get the lunch things?' Auntie asked.

'Good idea. It's a peach of a day! Let's have a picnic up here on the lawn' Uncle glanced down at the deck. 'That grass could do with a cut,' he said, shaking his head. 'I was meaning to do it a couple of days ago. Never got round to it though. Fetch the mower up, will you, when you're down there?'

'Oh you silly man. *I'll* mow the lawn. You concentrate on showing the children all of the toys you've got on your so-called *boat*. Perhaps you could let them have a go at driving it! It won't take me ten minutes to mow the deck. We'll have lunch afterwards.'

'Before you go, have a look at this,' Uncle passed a strip of paper to Auntie. It looked like the same one Charlie had seen printing out of the ticket machine before.

She quickly read the series of dots and gave it back.

'Better do what he says then,' she said.

'*Reel 'em in and lay low for a while.* This could be fun. Who wants a go at drivin'?' Uncle asked.

'Reel who in?' asked Charlie.

'Don't worry about that. It's Guardian, er … team business. You can go first, Charlie.'

'Wait a minute. Are you sure Mum and Dad are safe? I mean, those men might still be there,' Poppy said.

'They'll be fine. They couldn't be safer.' Uncle seemed keen to change the subject back onto the features of the floating bus.

'The vessel is bein' controlled through a series of computers what manages and guides her: *float by wire* I call it. If you try to steer her into water that ain't deep enough, or an obstacle, she has a little moan about it first and then she stops so as not to cause any damage.'

He left the helm and Charlie watched the steering wheel continue to make minor movements. It was keeping the bus on a perfectly straight course, all by itself.

'Go on, Charlie. In you get.'

Charlie sat down in the soft driver's seat.

'What are all these gauges, Uncle,' he asked, 'on your Tradget?'

'Well that 'uns your speed, 3.7 knots. The speed limit is five miles an hour, so you're fine. Here's your compass, still proceedin' in a westerly direction. Can't go too far east, there's a low bridge that way. That 'uns your depth, 1.6 metres at the moment, but if you keep watchin' that gauge you'll see summat odd happen in a minute.'

'*Something odd?* Surely not!' Rhodri said.

Charlie quickly got used to driving the bus. It was just

109

like riding a bike but with handlebars made out of very bendy rubber. The direction didn't change until a few moments after he'd moved the wheel.

'This is brilliant!' he said. 'I've never driven a boat before, or a bus! What's that big box on the end, with all the buttons on?'

'That's the most important device on the bus!' Uncle replied.

'What is it?' Rhodri asked. 'No wait, don't tell me. Is it some kind of satellite tracking equipment, or a radar? Maybe even a remote control for your gyrocopter?'

'No. It's the ticket machine. Not much point havin' a bus unless you can sell tickets, is there!'

'What are the things it keeps printing out?' Charlie asked.

'Just little messages, from me friends back in the village.'

'But why are they in that weird code, with all those dots?'

'Oh, it's just an old-fashioned piece of kit. It can't do modern messages with pictures and all that fancy stuff.'

As the boat came around a gentle curve in the river, Uncle seemed keen to draw everyone's attention back to the gauges.

'Watch that depth now,' he said.

Charlie watched the depth gauge. 'It's showing the river is about two metres deep.'

'That's right. Keep watchin' it.'

'I don't understand. Why is it suddenly showing over thirteen metres?' Charlie said. 'Isn't that over forty feet deep? That's deeper than a house, isn't it?'

'It is. I thought you said you were no good at Maths! This is the deepest non-tidal section of the river. There's a collapsed railway tunnel full of water down there. The Heinkel Hole they call it, after the type of plane that dropped the bombs that caused it to flood. If you look over there in that field, you can see a couple of craters where some of the other bombs landed.

'Was there a train in the tunnel?' asked Charlie.

'No. Funny thing is they knew the tunnel weren't safe, so it had been closed and was due to be demolished any-how. The bomber pilot did 'em a favour!'

'Can we go any faster?' asked Charlie.

'No! Five mile an hour is the limit. Any faster and our wake might damage the riverbank. Besides, folk that's fishin' don't like boats driving too quick and disturbin' 'em, and there's a lot of that on this section. They call this next bend Carp Corner. There's supposed to be a load of forty-pounders round there. Look at the Tradget display. Let's see if we can find any of 'em.'

Fishing? Charlie thought. *Reel them in*? He looked at the screen. It changed firstly to an image showing the weather and then to a cross-section of the river. It was almost as if they were looking through crystal clear glass and not the murky, brown river water.

'It's so clear,' Charlie said. 'Look, there are a load of old bottles and empty drinks cans. I can't believe the stuff people throw in the river.'

'Terrible, ain't it. Look, see them weeds? That's where the fish are hiding.' Uncle tapped the screen. 'There you go, kids. He's a big, ugly fella, ain't he?'

'Ooh, can we catch it for lunch?' asked Auntie, who

111

had returned onto the deck with a lawnmower.

Uncle laughed. 'I wouldn't eat that 'un! Maybe there'll be chance for a spot of fishin' later.'

'Yeah,– I'd love to have a go at fishing!' Charlie added. 'Maybe we could catch a few. You know *reel them in*. Then maybe we should, you know, *lay low*.'

'Right, Charlie, I think you've had long enough. Let one of the girls have a go at drivin'.'

'Go on, Poppy, you have a go,' Bryony said.

'What? I can't hear you!' Poppy replied, pointing towards her headphones.

'Don't worry, I'll go next!' Rhodri said, pushing in front of Bryony.

'Rhodri! You're not a girl though!'

'Oh come on, Rhodri, where are your manners? Ladies first and Bryony *has* been waiting so patiently,' Auntie said.

Rhodri stepped aside sheepishly.

'I thought we could set the table and chairs up at the front, just behind the helm, so we don't have to moor up for lunch. It's so much more enjoyable to have moving scenery, especially when it's this pretty!' Auntie said.

'Well if it wasn't pretty before, it is now!' Uncle was smiling at Auntie. She'd got changed into a very stylish summer dress, which was fluttering gently in the breeze.

No one spoke for a few seconds.

'Uncle?' Charlie asked.

'What is it?'

'Why *did* the those men try and shoot a rocket through your kitchen window?'

35

Mr and Mrs Crump had driven along a series of narrow, twisty lanes, to arrive in Great Disbury via a dusty track peppered with potholes. They parked their car behind the village shop, exactly as they had been instructed.

The curtains were closed on quite a few of the houses as they drove past.

'Where is everyone?' Mr Crump asked.

'This place gives me the creeps.' Mrs Crump said. 'Why did you ever even *think* of moving here? They're such an odd bunch, all they seem to care about is that daft quiz team.'

As Mr Crump looked over his shoulder at the pretty cottages, he remembered how he'd been told that moving to Great Disbury wasn't quite as easy as people seemed to think. *You can't just move here willy-nilly, you have to be invited. And anyway, you're still far too young. You'd soon get bored of the conversations about cricket, gardenin', politics and bowlin'!*

Godfrey Blessings appeared, seemingly from nowhere, and rapped on the car window with his gloved hand.

'You made me jump!' Mr Crump said, rubbing his head where he'd banged it on the ceiling. 'My brother-in-law sent us here ... seemingly for our er ... protection.'

'Yes, I've been expecting you,' Godfrey Blessings replied. 'You'd better hide your car in the garage.' He turned back towards the Post Office without saying another word.

Mr Crump noticed a rickety-looking double garage attached to the side of the shop. He started to get out of his car to open the weather-beaten doors.

'Don't bother trying to unlock the doors,' Godfrey Blessings shouted, without turning around. 'They won't open from the outside. Just stay in the car and start her up.'

The doors suddenly opened and, instead of swinging outwards as Mr Crump had expected, they disappeared very rapidly downwards, into the ground.

'Are you sure this is a good idea?' Mrs Crump asked.

'You heard him: "you'd better hide your car in the garage," he said.'

Before Mr Crump had moved forwards by more than a few feet, his car made a beeping sound and a voice spoke from somewhere underneath the dashboard.

'GUARDIAN MODE ARMED,' it said.

'What was that?' he asked.

Mrs Crump shrugged.

Shortly afterwards, it beeped again.

The rear-view mirror wobbled a few degrees in either direction, before snapping all the way around to face towards the open doors. The headlights of the car came on by themselves and illuminated the interior of the garage.

Mrs Crump gasped.

'What on earth is this?' she said.

Instead of lighting up the inside of a garage, the two pencil beams of light projected way into the distance.

Immediately in front of them, a set of sequenced lights had begun flashing, indicating the centre of a very long, straight road.

The car suddenly accelerated, racing away at a speed which clearly surprised Mrs Crump.

'Slow down,' she screamed. 'You're driving way too fast!'

'I can't!'

Large objects flashed past them on either side, which seemed to include a selection of military vehicles and a lot of large mechanical components. There were even some things that looked like jet engines and other aircraft parts.

'Did you know any of this was here?' Mr Crump asked, his head pressed hard back against the headrest.

Mrs Crump was gripping the side of her seat very tightly. 'No!' she gasped. 'I knew he liked military vehicles, but I had no idea he had all this!'

'There must be thousands and thousands of pounds worth here. Wherever did he get the money?'

'I don't know. The farm certainly doesn't bring …' she paused; the car seemed to be rapidly approaching a solid wall. '… that much money in.' She hurriedly finished her sentence, pushing her feet hard against the floor, as if she were trying to apply some imaginary brakes.

The car swerved to the right and stopped. Mr and Mrs Crump both groaned as their seat belts dug into their laps and chests.

They were in a large, open space, like the inside of a small, brightly lit warehouse. There were two levels with ramps leading up to what appeared to be parking spaces for about fifteen or twenty cars, like a small multi-storey car park.

There was another vehicle facing towards them. An old Morris Minor, with an exceptionally large number of shiny badges attached to the front grille. From what Mr Crump could make out, it was in immaculate condition, gleaming black, and looked like it had been polished for entry into a car show. It had a small, pulsing purple beacon on the roof.

Mr Crump's car had come to a halt alongside it. The door opened and Godfrey Blessings stepped out, leaving his own engine running.

Mr Crump opened his door and started to get out.

'Wow! That was quite a journey. I didn't realize I was such a good driver!'

'You're not,' replied Godfrey Blessings. 'It wasn't you driving that car, it was me.'

'What? But you were driving *your* car!' Mr Crump replied.

'I was driving them *both*.' Mr Blessings flicked his thumb towards the inside of his car, as if to draw attention to the strange, double steering wheel and larger-than-normal number of pedals and gear sticks protruding from the floor. 'You see that GB sticker on the back of your car? That means it's one of mine. I can drive it whenever I want, without asking; don't even need the keys. I take it this is your first time down here?'

'Er, yes. What is this place?' Mr Crump asked.

'Can't tell you too much about it I'm afraid. You have to be in our team to know the answer to that one.'

'But why are we here?' asked Mr Crump. 'We heard

Drakepuddle was being attacked.'

'It was. They've gone now. You're here for your own safety and we can get you out of here quickly if we need to. You're here until the aggressors have been flushed out and caught.' Mr Blessings replied. 'You may as well make yourselves comfortable. There's a lift up to the farmhouse over there,' he said, indicating an old, red telephone box in a corner of the parking area. I've got to go back to the Post Office now. It's pension day and I don't want to keep the old folks waiting. Oh, and it would be best if you never tell anyone about this place.' Godfrey Blessings got back into his car. Before he drove off, he opened the window. 'Remember, don't tell *anyone*,' he said, 'even your kids.'

The engine roared and the tyres of the black car squealed. Mr Crump watched flames spit out from the exhaust pipes, either side of the boot of the gleaming old car, as it shot off, whining like a racing car and fading into the distance. Within a few seconds, only the faint smell of burning rubber and petrol indicated that Godfrey Blessings had ever been in the tunnel.

'But what about the children?' Mrs Crump asked.

'Didn't you hear him? He said don't tell anyone.'

'No, I mean, how do we know *they're* safe?'

36

Uncle was pointing at an image of the lounge at Drake-puddle Farm. 'See, I told you your mum and dad would be safe,' he said.

Charlie watched his father reading the newspaper and his mother pacing up and down inside the room.

'Can we speak to them?' he asked.

'Tell you what, after lunch I'll patch us through and you can all have a good old natter,' Uncle replied. 'No point callin' 'em now anyway, there's no phone signal.'

Charlie looked at the old car windscreen. It too had lots of information projected onto it, including a picture of a telephone with a red cross through it. There was also a picture of something which looked like a satellite. Charlie noticed, it also had a red cross, which kept flickering on and off.

'Does that mean no one can get hold of us? Are we out of range?'

'Don't worry. Anythin' really important always gets through,' Uncle said, tapping the ticket machine, 'and we can still see 'em, can't we?'

*

Mrs Crump walked to the window. She looked at her watch and sighed heavily. 'I wish there was something we could do.'

Mr Crump threw the newspaper down onto his lap. 'Look, will you stop worrying! He'll know we're here. Poppy and Charlie are safe. They're with him on that bus thingy.'

'But we can't just sit around here and do nothing. What if whoever attacked this place is after Pip? They might go after him and, like you said, he's with the children.'

'But you heard him, "Go to Drakepuddle and stay inside".'

'I'm going to phone him. Perhaps we can speak to the children, to check they're alright.'

She picked up the telephone and dialled.

'Hello?' she said. 'Hello, it's—'

'Is it on? Oh, I'm not here now. I was when I said this, but because you're hearin' me say this, it means that I'm not here anymore. Well, I might be here, or I might be here but busy, or I might not be busy bu— Oh, it doesn't matter. Anyhow, just leave a message after the beep or ping, or whatever it is.'

Mrs Crump began talking, 'It's me. We're at the farm, like you said, but we're worried about the children, very worried.'

*

'Where's she going now?' Charlie asked, looking at the monitor.

'Probably just a bit fed up! I ain't got a telly at Drakepuddle. Don't worry about it. She can't come to any harm where she is. Safest place for 'em!'

'You don't think they'll go outside, do you? What if those men are still there?'

'They *ain't* still there. Hang on, look,' Uncle tapped

the screen and the display changed. 'See them heat sources? Your mum, your dad and four cats. Morgan's prob'ly gone huntin' for rabbits. If I zoom out more ... Look. Yep, there he is, down by the stream, and there's Nosebag. And see, them 'uns cows, them 'uns ducks, them 'uns chickens and them 'uns ... urrgh – *rats!* Come on, Charlie, back to fishin' for beer bottles. We're on holiday!'

*

The door to the room where Charlie and Rhodri had been sleeping was open, their unmade beds and a few of their belongings strewn across the floor. Mrs Crump closed the door and walked to the spiral staircase at the end of the landing.

She emerged into the stifling heat of the Ideas Room. *I can see why she calls it the greenhouse!* she thought.

One of the computer screens flickered into life and, almost immediately, the windows and a large central section of the ceiling roof light opened up. A desk fan started itself up and flew towards her, hovering just above her head, blowing cool air down on her and shielding her eyes from the sun.

As she stood next to the desk, looking out of the window, a robin landed on the branch of a nearby tree.

'What are you so chirpy about? It's okay for you,' she said quietly. 'You never have to worry about your children, you can just ...' She slapped her hand against her forehead. 'Of course!'

She spun around towards the fireman's pole and slid down it, landing heavily on the bedroom floor. She hurried to the lounge, almost tripping over in the doorway.

Mr Crump was still in his armchair, slumped over the newspaper, snoring.

'Perfect!' she whispered to herself as she walked softly to the corner of the room. She opened the door to the telephone box and stepped inside the lift.

Why didn't I think of this before?

There were four buttons. The first was marked *HERE* and was lit up in red. The second was marked *PLUS ONE*. And there was also a *MINUS ONE* and a *MINUS TWO*.

She pressed the button marked *MINUS TWO*.

The glass of the telephone box suddenly became opaque but Mrs Crump didn't move.

Some words appeared on a screen.

NOT AUTHORISED. GUARDIAN ACCESS ONLY

She waited for a moment and pressed the button marked *MINUS ONE*. This time she became light on her feet and felt a strange floating sensation in her stomach.

The doors opened and she stepped out of the telephone box into the deserted parking area.

The car wasn't locked.

Good!

She removed the large holdall, placed the straps over her shoulder and walked back to the lift. The holdall was surprisingly light considering its size, so she carried it with ease past her snoring husband and up to the attic room.

She placed the holdall on the floor, next to the desk and read the label.

QT FITCHETT & CO. LICENSED ENGINEERS

How difficult could it be?

She unzipped the holdall and emptied the contents onto the floor.

If a little creature like that can do it.

A large laminated card was tied to the frame of the contraption. She turned it over and read the big, boldly written words:

PAC 1-11VG MILITARY / EMERGENCY
SERVICES JETPACK
PROTOTYPE
**WARNING: EXPERIMENTAL FLYING
MACHINE**
CONSULT INSTRUCTION MANUAL BEFORE
USE

37

'Ain't you gonna wave at 'em?' Uncle asked. He was looking towards the riverbank.

Charlie turned around. Quite a large group of people had gathered outside a busy pub. As he watched, more and more people spilled out, to check if the story, which had been circulating inside, was true.

'Afternoon!' Uncle called out across the river to the crowd. 'Beautiful day, ain't it!'

Charlie raised his hand slightly so it was level with his waist and moved it hesitantly from side to side. It wasn't really a wave; not even half a wave. No one on the riverbank returned the gesture. Charlie noticed many heads shaking in disbelief, and a great many more that weren't moving at all. They were simply gawping at him. There was a lot of pointing too, but there was definitely no waving.

'They ain't a very friendly bunch, are they?'

'They probably think there's something wrong with the beer!' Rhodri added.

'What?' Charlie asked.

Rhodri turned his head towards Auntie, who was pacing carefully along the deck. The shiny, red lawnmower was putt-putting gently along in front of her.

Charlie smiled. 'Maybe they've never seen anyone mowing the roof of a bus before!'

'A bus with a small helicopter on top,' Poppy added.

'And *especially* not one being driven along the river *by a dog!*' Rhodri said, nodding towards the front of the deck.

Charlie looked.

Rhodri was right! Doris had jumped up into the driver's seat and was resting her front paws on the large steering wheel and panting contentedly.

'She looks like she's laughing!' Poppy said.

'She's just enjoyin' herself, ain't you, Doris? More than can be said for that miserable lot. Oh well, nowt so queer as folk!'

Auntie released the lawnmower handle and the engine spluttered and stopped.

'There we go. Good enough to play bowls on!' she said 'Oh, and I've got a little surprise for lunch! Poppy, could you come and give me a hand downstairs?'

'Surprise?' said Rhodri. 'What *sort* of surprise?'

Auntie tapped the side of her nose and turned towards the stairs.

Charlie turned back to the crowd on the riverbank. He noticed that one of the men watching wasn't pointing at the bus and there was something about him that looked familiar. Charlie noticed that his uncle was watching the man too.

He wasn't talking to the people around him outside the pub or shaking his head in disbelief either. He wasn't really doing anything.

Anything except watching the bus and, it seemed, talking … into a flask.

38

Mrs Crump read the last line of the printed warning again:

CONSULT INSTRUCTION MANUAL BEFORE USE.

She thought about the words for a few moments. It hadn't looked *that* complicated when she'd seen the instruction manual on the kitchen table.

She slung the jetpack over her shoulders and did up the fasteners.

'Just like putting on a rucksack and going for a nice walk,' she said aloud. 'Picnic blanket, sandwiches, a few cakes, nice flask of tea, jetpack.'

She climbed clumsily onto the desk and stood under the open roof light.

Her eyes scanned the contraption, looking for a switch to start it. The only thing she could find was a yellow and black striped handle at the front of the frame. It had a red tag with the words 'REMOVE BEFORE FLIGHT' written across it. She pulled the handle out.

It was like she'd pulled the pin out of a hand grenade. The room was filled by a series of, almost deafening, mechanical clattering and hissing sounds. The device had come to life so forcefully, she felt like she was being pushed in several directions at once by a dozen or so very strong robots.

'Oh my!' she said.

The force of the jetpack adjusting itself made her wobble. She thought she was going to lose her balance and topple backwards off the table. Instead, she remained perfectly upright, as if the strong robots were now holding her very, very still. She became quickly aware that this wasn't some kind of toy contraption, but a very powerful military machine. Somehow, she'd become part of a large mechanical monster. A monster which, she realized, she had frighteningly little control over. She stood motionless on top of the desk for a while amongst several swirls of mist that had emerged from some of the machine's joints and pipes.

Just as she realized that she had made a dreadful mistake, an authoritative, automated voice spoke.

'T MINUS TWENTY SECONDS,' it said.

Then shortly afterwards:

'T MINUS FIFTEEN SECONDS. GUIDANCE SYSTEMS ARMED.'

39

The bus had stopped at the moorings at Pigeonhome Park. Uncle had suggested stopping for a while to let Doris go for her afternoon walk, so Charlie and Rhodri had taken her for a stroll along the grassy bank.

'Did you see that man outside the pub earlier?' Charlie asked.

'Which one? There were at least a hundred.'

'The one talking into a flask. I saw him when we were leaving Drakepuddle too, just before it was attacked. And did you see any of that weird writing on the windscreen of the bus? It said he had a transmitter.'

'Yeah, I wondered what that was. So you reckon that guy with the flask might have something to do with the attack at your uncle's farm?'

'Well, I find out there's been a break-in at the Ministry of Defence and it could put everything and everyone at risk. Then I see a man talking into a secret transmitter and Drakepuddle is attacked, which happens to be where my uncle, who happens to be a secret weapons inventor lives, and I hear him mutter something about the Minatauri whilst it's all going on. Not only that, but Allsop goes missing, maybe because of something I took from my uncle. Then I see the same man, and he's talking into a flask again. I know I'm no Maths ace, but even I can put two and two together. Something's going on here and we're right in the middle of it.'

'But look, if someone *is* after your uncle, he isn't exactly making himself difficult to find. Just look at that.' Rhodri pointed to the bus.

'I know, but he keeps getting these printouts. You must have noticed. And did you hear him say what one of them meant? Reel 'em in.'

'What do you mean?'

'I mean I reckon he's setting a trap to flush out the Minatauri, and he's using himself as the bait!'

'Well, if he's the bait, what does that make us?'

40

For the fifth or sixth time that day, the inspector read the note. It was from Allsop. It had been tucked inside a lost wallet which a kind old man with watery eyes and a walking frame had handed in.

> *I am okay. This man hasn't*
> *hurt me yet. I miss all*
> *of my family. Give the*
> *formula and anyone's*
> *worry slips away, but*

as he is willing to go
any length to find it
TIME is the KEY

He handed the note to his colleague. She studied it carefully.

'It's written in a very strange way for a twelve-year-old boy!' she said, '*Anyone's worry slips away?*' And what are those noughts and crosses, scribbled around the edge?'

'I know, it's all very strange,' replied the inspector, 'Almost as if he's trying to tell us something.'

'Like what?'

'If only we knew! We've got a team of cryptanalysts — codebreakers — working on it. So far it's a total mystery.'

41

'Uncle, we need to speak to you,' Charlie said.

'You sound worried. Is summat troublin' you?'

'You could say that!' Rhodri began. 'One of the kids in our class goes missing and you're house gets shot up by …' He was interrupted by an alarm coming from somewhere on the bus.

'What the blazes?' Uncle said.

'What is it?' Charlie asked.

Uncle ripped a slip of paper from the ticket machine

and translated it out loud. '1-11VG jetpack activated, fifty-one degrees, fifty-three minutes north, Drakepuddle Farm!'

'What is it?' Rhodri said.

'The jetpack's been activated!'

*

'Er, Piddle on the Pew,' Mrs Crump said nervously, trying to remember where Uncle had said he would be taking the children.

She looked up through the open roof. The jetpack was holding her perfectly motionless, like she was paralysed from the neck down.

'THINKING,' the automated voice said.

'DESTINATION NOT RECOGNIZED. TRY AGAIN,' it added.

'River Pew,' Mrs Crump said, this time speaking more clearly and slowly.

'DESTINATION NOT RECOGNIZED. TRY AGAIN.'

'River,' she paused, giving the machine time to think. 'Pew.'

'THINKING. RIVER PEW. CONFIRM OR STATE NEW DESTINATION.'

'Yes! River Pew. Take me to it!'

'NEW DESTINATION TTOQQORTOORMMIT, GREENLAND IDENTIFIED.'

MISSION ACCEPTED.

PRIMARY WARNINGS: INSUFFICIENT FUEL.

SECONDARY WARNINGS: NUMEROUS.

LAUNCHING IN THREE ... TWO ... ONE ...'

*

'I don't believe it! Someone's flippin' launched it!'

'What is it?' Charlie asked.

'Someone's launched the jetpack, and I think it's … your mum! By the look of it she's set it up to fly to … Oh my giddy aunt! … *Greenland!*'

'No! What can we do?'

'Oh no, will she be okay?' Bryony asked. 'This is becoming one *very* strange day.'

'You're telling me!' Rhodri added.

'Do something!' Charlie yelled.

'I'm thinkin'!' Uncle replied. 'Where's Poppy's music player thingamajig? It might have a shortwave radio tuner.'

'A what?' asked Charlie.

'Just run downstairs and get her music thingy, quick as you can!'

Charlie almost knocked Auntie over as he stumbled down the stairs.

'Careful, Charlie!' she said. 'These are Dyna-Can-'

'Can't stop. Poppy. Music player. Where?' Charlie spluttered.

'Over there.'

He didn't wait for Auntie to finish her sentence. He spotted Poppy swaying from side to side at the back of the bus, singing along to one of her songs.

He ripped the music player from her hand. The headphone lead separated from the gadget and the song continued playing over a small, tinny-sounding speaker.

'Hey that hurt, you little—' Poppy began.

'No time! Mum — Jetpack — Greenland!'

'What? Mum? Greenland?' Poppy chased Charlie

towards the stairs and Auntie followed.

Charlie emerged onto the deck with the music player in his outstretched hand, still blaring out the same tinny tune. Uncle immediately began dismantling it.

'Thank god for that,' Rhodri said when Declan O' Duff's voice distorted and slowed down before stopping altogether.

'Aha! It *does* have a shortwave tuner. She's out of range for VHF, but I reckon I can contact the device on HF, even if I have to super-refract the signal.' Uncle announced.

'*What?*' Rhodri was the first to ask.

'Bounce a signal off the atmosphere to communicate with the on-board receiver in the apparatus. Pass us them pliers will you, Charlie.'

Charlie picked up a pair of pliers from a small toolbox, which his uncle had got from somewhere and put on the driver's seat.

'Er, I don't want to bother you,' Poppy said.

'No bother at all. I can fix your music thingy after-wards,' Uncle said, twisting some wires together and fiddling with some knobs on the dashboard of the bus.

'It's not that,' Poppy said.

'Uncle! We might need to …' Charlie started.

A lot of crackling and whistling started playing over the loudspeaker as Uncle rotated a dial.

'Don't worry, we've got —' Uncle looked at the flashing red message on the screen, 'almost four minutes till she runs out of fuel; I don't know if I'll be able to get Dougal O' Dud back though.'

The whistling and crackling turned into Morse Code,

131

then some people talking in a foreign language.

'Er ...' Poppy pointed over Charlie's shoulder towards the riverbank. She was interrupted by Auntie before she could finish her sentence.

'There we go. *Proper* music.'

'Uncle!' Charlie shouted, pointing to the riverbank too. 'Those men over there, walking towards us; aren't they the people who tried to break into your house?'

42

'Good god!' Uncle picked up his binoculars. There was no doubt: the men approaching along the riverbank *were* dressed in the same black clothing as the men who had attempted to break into Drakepuddle.

He didn't take the binoculars away from his eyes. 'They got here quicker than I thought,' he said quietly.

'What? You *knew* they'd come after us?' Poppy said.

'Get downstairs! NOW! First seat you can find, and get your seat belts done up ... tight!'

'B-b-but what about Mum?' Charlie asked.

'You stay here with me, Charlie. The rest of you downstairs.' He pulled the binoculars away from his face and turned to the other three children. '*NOW!*'

Charlie watched Poppy, Bryony and Rhodri scramble down the stairs.

'W-w-what do you want *me* to do?' he asked.

Uncle didn't say anything. He gave the binoculars to

Charlie and slid the driver's seat as far back as it would go so he could stand up behind the steering wheel.

Charlie looked into the distance through the binoculars. It took him a moment to find the boats. There were two of them: speedboats. He could make out the silhouettes of two or three men standing on each of them, and the way they were dressed looked very much like the men he'd seen trying to break into his uncle's house.

Uncle pressed a button and all the lights on the instrument panel lit up momentarily and the engine started.

'Hold on, Charlie. I need you to help me tune this radio in.'

Without bothering to undo the mooring lines, Uncle moved the throttle levers forward and the bus moved away from the riverbank, pulling the ropes taut and then snapping them.

Charlie noticed the men on the riverbank had started to run and he almost lost his balance as the bus accelerated towards the oncoming boats. As he regained his footing, he noticed his knees shaking. He knew it wasn't the bus. The river was calm.

'You're pointing straight at them!' he yelled.

Uncle turned the wheel sharply to the right and checked his instruments. 'Four green lights and one amber,' he said. 'Three kiddies, one wife and a dog. Good enough!' He increased the power and the bus performed a sharp U-turn on the river, leaning over at a very steep angle and leaving an impressive curved wake in its trail.

Almost immediately, Charlie heard a booming sound from behind. Something whistled through the air. He looked over his shoulder.

'They're getting closer!' he shouted.

A plume of water erupted into the air in front of the bus, soaking both Charlie and his uncle with spray.

'You holdin' on tight?' Uncle asked.

Charlie nodded. He was holding on tight all right. No way was he falling off that bus into the river, into the path of those speedboats.

He glanced over his shoulder again. They were getting closer. There was a puff of smoke from the front of one of the boats, followed by another boom.

Something hissed through the air. He couldn't see it, but whatever it was sounded close; *very* close.

Uncle moved the throttle levers further forward and the front of the bus lurched upwards then bounced back into the river, sending large splashes of water out to either side. This happened three or four times until the splashing stopped and the ride became much smoother.

'We're up on the front hydrofoils now,' Uncle said. 'That large dial on the left is the signal tuner. You're going to need to connect the transmitter to the bus's power supply first though.'

'What? I can't do that!'

'It's easy. Underneath the ticket machine, there's a small hatch. Open it.'

Another huge plume sprayed into the air slightly to the right of the bus, even closer than the last one.

Charlie opened the small hatch. There were hundreds and hundreds of cables and wires.

'Inside you'll see a load of wires,' Uncle said.

He wasn't kidding, Charlie thought. There had to be at

least 500 wires.

'There's a hexagonal-shaped junction box, about two-thirds of the way down. It should have a red and green striped wire coming out of it.'

'Hexagonal what?' he said, glancing behind. Immediately, he wished he hadn't. 'They're still gaining on us!' he shouted before turning his attention back to the bewildering selection of wires and boxes crammed inside the small hatch.

'I was hopin' we could outrun 'em on two hydrofoils. Hang on to summat, Charlie. We need more power.'

Uncle slammed the throttles fully forwards. The bus lurched again. Charlie started to slide towards the back of the deck. He grabbed hold of the first thing he could; a handful of the wires.

It wasn't a good feeling. He was soaking wet and he had a fistful of electrical wires, but it was better than falling into the river and being hit by one of those boats … or worse. As if that wasn't bad enough, his mum was still whizzing over the countryside on an uncontrollable jetpack as well.

His eyes darted around, looking for something better to hold on to.

There was nothing.

His free arm scrabbled around for something to grab hold of.

The only thing he could reach was the open door of the hatch, but his wet hands had no grip at all on the smooth plastic door.

'How much time have we got,' Charlie asked, 'to save Mum?'

Uncle glanced at the screen. He tapped it.

'You ain't pullin' them wires yet, are you? If you pull the wrong 'un out, we'll have no chance of transmittin' to her. As it is, we've got …' the tone of his voice changed, '… about a minute.'

About a minute? That wasn't enough time!

Charlie heard three or four hisses and several small waterspouts shot from the wet deck a few feet in front of him. The unmistakeable sound of a bullet ricocheting off something brought Charlie's thoughts back into focus.

He kicked around blindly with his legs. There had to be something to stop him slipping backwards and pulling against the wires he was holding.

Anything would do.

Anything!

He found something solid.

It was the base of one of the seats.

He pushed down against it with his foot to slide himself forwards, as he did so, he felt the back of the bus start to rise out of the water.

Uncle glanced down at him. 'We're up on the rear hydrofoils too now.'

'H-h-how long? For Mum.'

Uncle seemed to ignore the question. Instead, he turned to the handrail next to the staircase. Auntie was pulling herself up onto the deck. What on earth was she doing?

She shouted something to Uncle.

'WHAT?' Charlie heard Uncle reply, above the noise of the water splashing over the side of the bus.

'ROCKETS!' Auntie shouted, 'ON JENNY. SHALL I START THE ROCKETS?'

Charlie pushed himself forwards. As he struggled to get to his knees, he caught sight of his uncle giving a thumbs-up sign to Auntie. He glanced at the screen where the flashing red words he saw made his heart miss a beat and sink through his stomach like it was a brick thrown into the river: *PAC 1-11VG JETPACK. LOW FUEL STATE. ENDURANCE: FORTY SECONDS.*

'Just get that red 'n' green wire, Charlie. But make sure you've got the one comin' out the hexagonal box. Don't touch anythin' coming out the pentagon-shaped box.'

'What's the difference?' Charlie asked. *Forty seconds! Forty seconds!*

'Don't matter. Just don't get the wrong box!'

Charlie looked over his shoulder again. The bus was still within range of the speedboats and there were quite a lot of flashes coming from their direction. Auntie seemed totally oblivious to the gunfire. He caught a glimpse of her walking towards the rear of the bus with one hand on the handrail. Her dress was flapping around her knees in the slipstream and her smart handbag was blowing around at the end of its strap, like an out-of-control kite.

For a split second he wondered what she was doing. A split second was all he could spare. Hexagon? Pentagon? Which was which?

It was almost as if someone was whispering the words in his ear.

Hex ends in x like six.

He found it. Just as he was about to pull the wire from the box, Charlie felt a burst of acceleration; he started to slide backwards again. Remembering the foothold of the seat, he managed to stop himself slipping along the deck.

He looked over his shoulder. Fierce blue flames roared out from either side of the gyrocopter. Auntie was sitting in the pilot's seat. Charlie noticed that it wasn't just him that was shaking. The entire bus was shuddering quite violently.

Through the hazy, shimmering rocket exhaust, Charlie noticed the speedboats starting to fall behind into the distance.

'Connect the wire to the positive terminal in the music player! The one with the plus sign on it!'

Charlie didn't waste any time, noticing that the ride had suddenly got a lot smoother, the hydrofoil legs had folded outwards, and were now acting like small, stubby wings. The bus was flying. Only a few inches above the river admittedly, but it was definitely flying. Not a single part of it was touching the calm water.

'Now look for a purple lead and—'

The instruction was interrupted by a loud, repeating chime and a mechanical voice: 'WARNING: FUEL STATE.'

'Any purple lead, Charlie. And hurry! Connect it to the top of the earphone socket, not the inside.'

Charlie found a purple wire. He gave it a firm tug.

Nothing happened.

He pulled it again and twisted it.

Come on! Snap!

Still, nothing happened.

'WARNING: CRITICAL FUEL. MALFUNCTION IMMINENT.'

Charlie placed both hands on the wire and pulled and

twisted as hard as he could.

Snap! Come on. SNAP!

The wire came loose. Immediately another alarm sounded:

'TERRAIN, TERRAIN.'

What had he done? He was sure he'd found the hexagonal box and he checked the colour of the loose wire in his hand. It was definitely purple!

'Was that me?' he called to Uncle.

'No. There's a bridge comin' up. We can't fly over it. Touch the wire on the headphone socket. QUICK!'

'Are we going to hit the bridge?'

'JUST TOUCH THE WIRE!'

'Okay, done it.' Charlie said.

Uncle jabbed down hard on a button. 'Abort!' he commanded into the microphone.

'WARNING FUEL. TERRAIN, TERRAIN.'

'Abort. Abort.' Uncle shouted again.

'ABORT SIGNAL SENT. SCANNING HF FREQUNCIES …

NO RESPONSE: TERRAIN, TERRAIN, WHOOP WHOOP. TOO HIGH.'

'ABORT! ABORT! ABORT!' Uncle shouted into the microphone as he snapped the throttle levers back.

Charlie looked at the wire and pushed it as hard as he could against the headphone socket. His arms were shaking. This time, it wasn't fear making him tremble, but determination.

Sparks flew from the top of the music player.

Was it too late?

Charlie rolled forwards, almost falling into the open

hatch as the bus slowed rapidly.

'Damn it! ABORT!' Uncle shouted.

'ABORT SIGNAL SENT. FREQUENCY 11396 TUNED.'

Charlie noticed that his clothes were dripping. He'd thought at first it was water spray from the river, but it wasn't only that: he was sweating heavily. He looked up at Uncle.

'Your mum's, okay, Charlie. Parachuting safely to earth as we speak!'

Charlie uncurled from the soggy bundle he had rolled himself into. As he started to stand up, he felt his uncle's hand on his shoulder.

'We're not out the woods yet, Charlie!'

'Did you say we can't get over that?' Charlie said, pointing at the bridge a few hundred feet ahead. He knew the speedboats were somewhere behind too, probably still racing after them at their top speed.

'That's right, Charlie, we can't!'

There was no way they could get under it. Charlie didn't need any clever measuring equipment to work out the bus was way too tall. He could see boats on the other side, moored up on the riverbank. And he wasn't looking at them *under* the bridge, he was looking *over* it.

He watched Uncle move a handle on a green, metal plate by his knee.

A siren sounded loudly throughout the bus.

AH – OOOOOOOOG – AH... AH – OOOOOOOOG – AH.

The section of the roof that housed the gyrocopter,

with Charlie's auntie still strapped inside, started to re-tract itself below the roofline.

Then the bike rack and bikes slid smoothly into the rear of the bus. Shortly afterwards, Charlie, his uncle and the first few rows of seats also started to lower them-selves inside the bus.

Lastly, the handrail, which formed the perimeter of the deck, and the windscreen from the old Rolls Royce, dis-appeared into the roof.

As he lowered beneath the deck, Uncle spoke into the microphone, 'Dive, dive, dive. Make our depth three zero feet.'

43

The roof clicked shut above Charlie's head. Poppy, Bryony and Rhodri were staring at him from their seats, their mouths wide open and, even if any of them had tried to speak, Charlie wouldn't have heard them anyway above the din of all the bells and sirens which screamed throughout the bus.

'It's alright,' Uncle said as the pandemonium subsided. 'Charlie's saved your mum. She'll have summat interestin' to tell the other dinner ladies when she goes back to work, eh? And I reckon your headmaster will be impressed by Charlie's bravery too.'

'Well, I think that's enough excitement for one day!' Auntie said, straightening the lines of her dress.

'Er, excuse me, Mr Clunckle,' Rhodri asked, scanning around through the darkening windows, 'but is this bus sinking?'

'Best we hide out the way of them clowns, till we think it's safe. We can stay down here for a while.'

Poppy had been looking out of the window, watching the gloomy, brown water rise up past the upper deck. Hundreds of bubbles streamed up to the surface.

'Hide down here? In a bus? How long are we going to hide down here?' she asked. 'And who are those people? First they try and break into your house, then they chase us down the river.'

Uncle turned away. 'Blimey, it is murky. We'll be well hidden down here. Probably don't need to lay low for too long, only a day or two.'

'*A day or two?* There's no way I'm spending a night on this bus down here surrounded by fish, weeds and … and … *duck poo!*'

'It ain't that bad down here. It's a bit like bein' in a big bath!' Uncle replied.

'I think it will be quite cosy, I can cook us a nice dinner and your uncle will light the fire. We can all sit around playing board games. Have you played Inane Insane Brain Strain? It's really rather fun. And we'll make your uncle be the banker, so he doesn't win all the time,' added Auntie.

'You spoilsport!' protested Uncle.

'Sit around?' Charlie said. 'What about finding out what's happened to Mum? or Allsop?'

'I can't even listen to my music. This is turning into the most vile holiday *EVER!*' Poppy stormed off to the rear of the bus and locked herself in the toilet.

'Actually, I think it's the coolest holiday I've ever had!' said Rhodri.

'Wait a minute.' Charlie said. 'We still don't know where Mum is, and how do we know *we're* safe?' added Charlie.

'Yes, and why are they after you? And why don't we tell the police? There must be *something* they can do. They could keep your house safe, at least,' Bryony said.

'I'm sure someone will have reported an armed boat chase to 'em and I've told you, Drakepuddle is ... 'ang on. I think those jokers are coming back.' He pointed to two flashing dots on the Tradget screen. 'Bandits, six o'clock. High!'

'Six o'clock high?' Charlie questioned.

'It's clock code. It means they're directly behind us ... and above us.'

'Well, they're hardly going to be *below* us,' Rhodri added.

The two speedboats passed overhead.

'Could they find us with sonar, like in the films?' Charlie asked.

'Not a chance! I've got eight layers of stealth paint on this bus and acoustic confusers on all the corners. Don't worry. You're safe down here. We've got more chance of being caught by a fisherman than being found by those twits.'

'But who are they? And where's my mum?' Charlie asked.

'Don't worry about your mum. I managed to use the last couple of seconds of fuel to launch her on a trajectory towards the police station. Her parachute landed right in the middle of the police car park. Probably gave 'em a right shock!'

Charlie's auntie giggled. 'She's probably nattering away to the duty sergeant having a nice cup of tea and a sticky bun as we speak.'

'But who are they? Why are they chasing us?'

'I reckon they're after me. They must think I've got summat they want. Looks like that floating circus up there just got bigger. Look.' Uncle pointed at the display again.

'Now what are they doing?' asked Rhodri.

'It looks like someone is chasing *them* now. And by the look of it, they have help from above. See that blip there, with the numbers next to it, that's moving like a helicopter?'

'Do you think they've got a helicopter to look for us?' asked Charlie.

'Depends what you mean by *they*. I reckon that's a police helicopter.'

'What? Now the police are looking for *us?*' asked Bryony, sounding worried.

'Well, they might want to have a word with us about flying down the river at a 150 miles an hour, I'll have speak to 'em about that later.'

'But those men were shooting your bus!'

'I know. I expect they're much more interested in catching 'em for shooting machine guns and firing rockets on the river, but exceedin' five mile an hour is against the rules too.'

*

Later that evening, whilst Uncle was trying to repair Poppy's music player, Charlie approached Auntie who was doing the washing-up.

'Do you want a hand with that?' he asked.

'Oh, thank you. Can you put those cups away, your uncle hasn't got round to installing a wishwasher on the bus yet.'

He took the medal he had found in the old uniform and put it on the table.

'Has this got anything to do with those people chasing and shooting at us?' he asked.

'Where did you find that?'

'It was in an old uniform, in the loft room. It just fell out of one of the pockets.'

'It *fell* out?'

'It did, honestly.' Charlie knew he was close to being told that Auntie didn't need any help with the dishes. She was giving him that look again. 'So does it have anything to do with those men: the Minatauri?'

'He doesn't like to—'

'Don't tell me. He doesn't like to talk about that either.'

'Something you've got to understand, Charlie, is that a lot of what he did was, well … secret.'

'But this is the Victoria Cross. How did he get it?'

'He was part of a small team watching — I suppose you could say *spying* on —the Minatauri, trying to find out what equipment they had. His unit had been totally cut off for days, with no food and their radio was broken. Your uncle led an attack to get some rations for his men. He came under heavy fire from them, but managed to get enough food and supplies to keep them all going, until they were eventually rescued.'

'But I had no idea Uncle had been given a medal. No one's ever mentioned it,' Charlie said.

'He doesn't feel like a hero.' Auntie put the tea towel down and lowered her voice. 'He hates war,' she said quietly. 'In fact, and he probably wouldn't want me to tell you this either, but every night before he goes to bed, he says a prayer—'

'For peace.' Neither Charlie nor his auntie had heard Uncle come down the stairs. 'I only did what anyone would've done.' He was looking at the medal on the table. 'I were no braver than anyone else. I was hungry. we were all hungry: bloomin' starvin'. Hadn't eaten for nearly five days. We were cut off and we could smell 'em cooking their food. Sausages; big, fat, juicy sausages. There were no shootin' or shellin', so all we could hear was the sizzlin' and poppin' of the sausages. I was prob'ly the hungriest, that's all. I weren't thinkin' straight.'

'But you saved all those men!' Charlie said.

'I only did what anyone else would've done. All that bloomin' medal does is remind me about all the killin' and death. That's why I don't wanna talk about it. I'd far rather it'd gone to a real hero, and one what hadn't hurt no one either.'

'But it's the Victoria Cross!' Charlie said, 'One of the highest medals for bravery you can get!'

Uncle was still staring at the medal. 'I know, Charlie, I know.'

44

The inspector stood before the assembled police officers.

'The kidnapper has been in touch again. This was found, stuck to the windscreen of an abandoned white van, like a parking ticket. It had my name on it.'

He unfolded a letter and read it aloud.

'*A sample of the substance must be delivered by hand to the left luggage office at Waterloo station before midday on this coming Monday, 1st August. I also want a precise list of its ingredient parts and details of its manufacturing process. The boy will not be released until the parcel has been delivered. Attempting to trace the package after it has been delivered will be futile. To prove the boy is well, I have enclosed another note from him.*'

He put the letter down.

'Just like the previous letter, there are no indications where the note came from. No watermarks, bog standard paper; can get it almost anywhere. No fingerprints. No forensic clues. Nothing!' He picked up a second piece of paper. 'It came with this,' he said.

He read Allsop's note:

'*I am still ok. I hope you will find me before 12 o' clock on the 1st.*'

It's been confirmed as being in his handwriting by the

boffins. They've compared it to his school books.'

'He's a bit arrogant, isn't he? I mean what does he mean tracking it *"will be futile"*? We could easily put a tracker on the package or employ a surveillance team at the station,' one of the police officers suggested.

'Can't we just make something up to deliver and follow him? By the time he's realized it's not the right stuff, we'll have followed him to his hiding place and found the boy,' added one of the other officers.

'Waterloo is the busiest station in London, and we've no way of knowing when he'll actually collect the package. We'd need a huge surveillance team,' the first officer said.

'I agree. We have to deliver something to Waterloo on Monday. Ideally the substance he wants. We have to make him … *or her* … think it's the genuine article.' Inspector Yarn turned to the officer who'd suggested tracking the package, 'There's a risk with your suggestion of following the package. What if he doesn't take it to the same place the boy is being held?'

'Good point. He could be anywhere.'

'Did the boffins make any sense of the boy's first note? The noughts and crosses?'

'They've been working on it, but they haven't found anything yet. It could be random doodles. The only common theme is that he started each game with a nought or a zero in the middle. It's not like any code they've ever seen before.'

Inspector Yarn walked to the front of the room and studied the photographs pinned to the wall.

'We've been interviewing his classmates and the staff

at the school, but it's the summer holidays. Most of them are away. One thing's for sure: we've got to do every-thing we can between now and Monday to come up with a way of saving that boy.'

45

Something woke Charlie the following morning. It sounded like something bumping softly against a window somewhere outside the bus.

'What's that?' he whispered quietly to anyone who might be awake.

There was no reply. He looked around. Doris was curled up asleep in her basket, next to the last fading embers of the fire.

'What's that? Can anyone hear it?' he repeated.

There was still no reply.

'Hello? Is anyone else awake?'

He heard the tapping again. This time it seemed clearer.

Knock, knock, knock

He got out of bed and rummaged around on the table, where he remembered there had been a torch.

'Rhodri? Is that you? Are you awake?'

He found the torch but, somehow knocked it onto the floor. He heard it roll away. He fumbled around blindly on his hands and knees, looking for it. Something made him stop. It was the knocking again. Three times. This time it was definitely louder.

KNOCK, KNOCK, KNOCK

Surely he couldn't be imagining it? It sounded as if it was coming from one of the windows just behind him. Still no one else on the bus stirred.

He groped around and managed to grab the torch.

He picked it up and found the rubber button on the top. He pointed it towards the window where he thought the noise was coming from. As soon as he switched it on, he realized he was holding it the wrong way round. It shone brightly in his face, blinding him for a moment. He quickly turned it around and probed each of the corners inside of the bus with the narrow beam of light.

Everyone appeared to be sleeping. He sat still for a minute or so. The noise seemed to have stopped.

It must have been a fish or some rubbish; maybe a drinks can floating along the bottom of the river and tapping against the side of the bus.

He got back into bed and closed his eyes. It was quiet again, apart from the loud snoring coming from the direction of Rhodri's bed.

He was just nodding off when, suddenly, he stirred.

Was that it again?

He got out of bed for a second time and walked to the window closest to where he thought the noise was coming from.

His heart was pounding fast and his pulse hammered in his ears — *BOOM-BOOM. BOOM-BOOM* — drowning out Rhodri's snoring

This was stupid; it was just a drinks can!

He moved his hand towards the curtains as if to open

them.

He changed his mind. There could be anything out there. He'd seen films where zombies that had drowned came back to life at night.

Come on, don't be such a coward! You rescued your mum yesterday, and you were being shot at!

He lifted his hand again, grabbed the bottom of the curtain and held it for a few seconds then he yanked it sharply to the side.

Nothing.

He shone the torch out through the window at arm's length. The beam only penetrated two or three feet through the murky water. Slowly, he moved his face closer to the window.

Nothing but cloudy, dark water. He pressed his head right up against the glass and searched around with the beam of the torch.

Still nothing.

Suddenly he jumped.

'What are you doing?'

'My god, you made me jump!' Charlie turned around. It was Rhodri. 'I thought I heard something outside, knocking on the window.'

'It was probably a fish or something. Give me that.' Rhodri snatched the torch.

He moved the beam slowly around through a wide sweeping arc and then back to the centre.

'See there's noth—'

'AAAAAAAAAAARGH!' they screamed together.

There, directly in front of them, through the murk, only a few inches away from their faces, in what looked to be a small glass bowl, was a pair of human eyes, staring at them.

46

Uncle jumped out of bed as soon as he heard the commotion.

'What? What's goin' on?' he asked.

'Th-th-there's someone outside,' Charlie said.

'We saw … some eyes … staring at us!' Rhodri added.

'What? Who the 'eck would be down here at,' he looked at his watch, 'seven o' clock in the mornin'?'

'I heard someone knocking on the window,' Charlie said.

'Don't be so bloomin' daft. Prob'ly just a fish or—' Before he could finish his sentence he was interrupted.

KNOCK, KNOCK, KNOCK

'Gimme that torch!'

Charlie gave the torch to his uncle.

On the other side of the glass, there was a whiteboard held up by a pair of hands. It had some writing on it:

IS THIS YOUR VEHICLE, SIR?

Uncle gave the torch back to Charlie and went to the desk. He scribbled something on a piece of paper, which he held up to the window.

YES. WE AR OK. WE WILL SURFISS THE BUS NOW. PS. SORRY ABOWT THE SPEEDIN.

The police diver turned to face his colleague. The two

exchanged some hand signals and disappeared into the
gloom.

Uncle walked towards the front of the bus and pulled
something from the ceiling next to the driver's position.
Charlie thought at first it was one of those periscopes that
bus drivers used to see if the kids on the top deck were
misbehaving, only it was clearly much more advanced.
There was some kind of small television screen
sandwiched between two handles.

'Looks like there's quite a welcomin' party up there.
Come on everybody, rise 'n' shine!'

*

Charlie stood near an open window, eating a bacon
sandwich and watching the policemen on the riverbank,
all of whom were examining the bus with a great deal of
interest. He was close enough to hear the conversation
between his uncle and one of the policemen.

'Sorry about that speedin' on the river. I were tryin' to
get away from some ... umm ... er ...'

'Terrorists?' suggested the senior policeman.

'Well, I was going to use another word, but I s'pose
you could call 'em that.'

'We've apprehended the *terrorists*. It was quite a chase
but we got them in the end. I'm afraid you're going to
have to come to the station, to give a statement.'

'I suppose I ain't got any choice. How did you find us
by the way?'

'There were quite a few witnesses, from outside a pub
a couple of miles up the river. The first one who came
forward claimed to have seen ...' the policeman licked
his finger and flicked through the pages of his notepad, *'a*

low-flying bus with a helicopter strapped to the roof with flames coming out the back, being chased by speedboats, whizzed past me after my fourth pint of Blunderblast . It looked like the same bus I saw earlier with a smartly dressed woman mowing the roof.' The policeman put the notepad back in his jacket pocket. 'We thought we were dealing with a timewaster at first, so we sent him home for a lie down, but then some more people came forward with a very similar version of events. No one saw the bus further down the river and no one saw it leave the river. We thought that there was only one place it could possibly be hiding if it was still *in* the river.'

'The Heinkel Hole!'

Uncle turned around to get back on the bus. He caught Charlie's eye.

'*Curious* state of affairs, eh?'

Charlie turned away and walked towards the back of the bus where Rhodri was throwing the crusts from his sandwich into the river for some ducks.

Terrorists? he thought. So that's who the Minatauri were, and now he *had* reeled them in.

47

Several policemen had gathered around the bus outside the police station.

'Funny way to catch a fish!' one of them joked.

Charlie could see the policeman's point. Both he and

Rhodri were on the pavement beside the bus. They each had buckets to catch the fish, which were being thrown off the roof by Auntie.

'Looks like they've finished questioning your uncle. Here he comes now, with your mum,' Auntie shouted.

As soon as his mum spotted him, she ran towards Charlie. Uncle followed close behind, accompanied by Inspector Yarn and Mr Crump.

'Oh! Thank you, Charlie! Your uncle told me what you did to save me.' She hugged Charlie so tight, he could barely breathe. 'And thank goodness you're okay. Where's Poppy?'

Charlie pointed towards the top of the bus. 'On the roof. Her and Bryony are lazing about in the sun.'

Uncle looked at Charlie's bucket.

'Caught any big 'uns yet?' he asked. 'They wanna have a word with you too, Charlie, about the boat chase,' he added.

'Me? What? I haven't done anything wrong.'

'It sounds to me like you've done everything *right*,' Inspector Yarn said. 'We just want you to see if any of you can identify any of them. I mean the men on the river. Apparently you had a good look at them.'

'B-b-but I ...'

'Don't worry, Charlie, they won't be able to see you,' the inspector said. 'Just a few questions and a look at a few mugshots, that's all.'

*

'The people who were chasing you were, we believe, from an organization called *the Minatauri*. They're being incredibly tight-lipped. We don't know if they're working by themselves or taking orders from someone else. All we know is they have some pretty advanced equipment.'

Yeah, Charlie thought, *the weapons thieves that had broken into the Ministry and tried to do the same at Drakepuddle; the same group that were behind what had happened to his uncle's parents.* No wonder he'd gone to such crazy lengths to flush them out.

'Why are they after us?' Rhodri asked, 'What do they want?'

'And will someone tell me why we're sat in this police station, having been chased and *shot at?*' Poppy's voice sounded almost tearful.

'It's 'cause of me.' There was a long pause whilst Uncle pulled out a chair and sat down at the inspector's desk. 'I had to get them to come after us. They're dangerous; a menace. They'll stop at nothin' to try and get hold of the most dangerous gear. I reckoned the safest way to keep 'em away from Drakepuddle was to get 'em to come after us. I knew they'd never catch us and there'd be a good chance they'd get caught 'emselves. And I've got good reason to want them banged up behind bars at long last.'

'But what do they want from you?' Charlie asked.

'They think I've got summat they want, but I don't do that stuff anymore though.' He tapped his fingers on the desk. 'Well, *hardly ever!*'

48

'Do you recognize any of these men?' Inspector Yarn placed about a dozen photographs on the desk.

'Yes, him. He was the man on the riverbank when we were moored up. Just before the boats appeared,' Charlie answered.

'Are you sure?'

'Positive. I recognize his eyes, and his hair. I saw him outside the Post Office in Great Disbury too. Poppy saw him on the riverbank, didn't you?'

'Yes, he was definitely on the riverbank,' Poppy said. 'I'd know those nasty eyes anywhere. He looks a bit like that awful judge on Cavernous and Ravenous. You know, the one that voted off Dec—'

'Okay, okay. We think he might be the leader. How about any of the others? What about any of the men on the boats?'

'They were too far behind us, I couldn't really see their faces,' Charlie answered. 'And I don't think he's the leader. He was speaking to someone else through a transmitter.'

'Yes, we found that. Are you sure you couldn't see any of the others' faces? Even with the binoculars?'

'No, sorry.' Charlie watched the inspector looking at the photographs and nodding his head. 'They were miles away and my mum was out of control—'

'Flying across the countryside with a jetpack strapped to her back, I know.'

There was a knock and a uniformed policewoman walked in carrying a piece of paper, which she handed to the inspector.

Inspector Yarn read it silently.

'Now about that speedin'. I know the limit is five mile an hour and I reckon I was doin' about thirty times that and technically, I think I broke most of the low-flyin' rules in the book too. So am I gonna get some points on me licence or anythin'?' Uncle asked.

Inspector Yarn put the piece of paper down. He looked up and frowned.

'I'm more concerned about putting these terrorists to rights and solving my other case: the one about that missing schoolboy. I'm a lot less worried about how the boating, or even flying laws apply to your er ... bus.'

'What missing boy? Allsop?' Charlie asked.

'You're at school with him, aren't you? I recognize your faces from the photos of his classmates.'

'Yeah, he's in our class,' Rhodri added. 'Is he still missing?'

The inspector put the piece of paper down on the desk and walked towards a large filing cabinet.

'We're trying to speak to all of his school friends, to see if they've got any idea what's happened to him.'

'We all *know* him, but let's not pretend,' said Bryony. 'He's so horrid and *vile* there's no way he's our *friend!*'

'Do you have *any* idea what might have happened to him?' the inspector removed a large envelope from the filing cabinet.

Charlie shuffled in his seat as Poppy fixed him with a knowing look across the table.

'The problem is whoever has him is demanding a sample of a substance: something that caused him to suffer some kind of meltdown and attack his teacher. We're appealing to anyone who might know anything about it.'

'I might be able to save you an awful lot of time,' Uncle said. 'That boy went potty because Charlie here stole some of my IQ-C_2. It was only a prototype. It wasn't ready to be tested by people, especially not kids.'

'What's IQ-C_2?' Inspector Yarn asked.

'It's a survival ration, dairy-based, with … Oh, it doesn't really matter. It's to help maintain mental performance, and tastes a bit like custard.'

'*What?* Are you telling me that boy has been kidnapped because he stole some *custard?*'

'Well, technically it's a survival ration.' Uncle scowled, 'It's still in the early stages of development, and I'm beginning to see why someone might want to get hold of it now.'

'You are?' enquired the inspector.

'They must think it could be used as a weapon, sendin' people senseless, mad as a minefield full of March hares! Problem is, it ain't supposed to do that at all.'

'Can you get us a sample?' Inspector Yarn asked. 'It's what he wants, in exchange for the boy's release.'

'No. I knocked a load of stuff on the floor and it all got mixed up. Like I said, it ain't supposed to send anyone cuckoo. I've no idea what was in the batch Charlie took. I can get you a batch of summat, but it won't be exactly the same as what that lad stole.'

'Wait a minute. How did Jasper Allsop get hold of it?' the inspector asked. 'I thought you said Charlie took it.'

Charlie was only too happy to explain the details of how he had taken the carton out of the Bovver-Upper recycling bins and taken it into school to impress Snitterborne, and how Jasper Allsop had then stolen it from him. The inspector already knew the rest of the story.

'By the way, there's something else. These came with the kidnapper's demands. They're notes from Jasper. We think he's trying to tell us something, but we're not sure what. They might be coded messages. Take a look.' The inspector showed the two notes that were in Allsop's handwriting to Uncle. He read them to himself two or three times and rubbed his chin.

'It's a bit weird ain't it? *Anyone's worry slips away?*'

'We know. It doesn't make much sense to us either.'

'Blimey O'Reilly. I thought my grammar were bad! And what are those noughts and crosses all about?'

'We don't know that either. Maybe he was just bored. I mean, a young lad kidnapped, probably with no books to read, no entertainment … he could easily just be doodling. His headmaster says he's always messing about; quite disruptive. The second note makes more sense,' said Yarn. 'See what you think.'

Uncle lowered his glasses and raised his eyebrows. He placed the first note on the table, right in front of Charlie.

Charlie read it to himself quickly:

I am ok. This man hasn't

hurt me yet. I miss all
of my family. Give the
formula and anyone's
worry slips away but
as he is willing to go
any length to find it
TIME is the KEY

He had a weird, familiar feeling. It was as if some rusty old wheels or something were turning slowly in his head. *Hasn't hurt me yet. Give the formula. Worry slips away. Length to find it. TIME is the KEY.*

Charlie noticed his uncle staring at him in a peculiar way and the rusty wheels slowly stopped turning and seized solid.

'Then there's this,' the inspector said. It came with the second note from Jasper's kidnapper. He's demanding we deliver your formula to Waterloo station by midday on the first of August.'

Uncle read the second note aloud.

'*I am still ok. I 'ope you will find me before 12 o' clock on the 1st.* It sounds a lot more normal, but I'm not sure he's trying to tell you anythin' He just hopes you find him before it's too late,' he said.

'So nothing particularly jumps out at you then, from his notes?'

'Can't say as it does. Does it mean anythin' to you?' he asked, looking at Charlie.

'No,' Charlie replied.

'You *sure?*' Uncle asked.

Even if he had managed to decode the message on the

postcard before, Charlie couldn't remember how, and he'd only been able to do it because he'd had a lot of help from his uncle. Hadn't he?

Charlie looked at the second note. There were no noughts and crosses, or doodles or scribbles on this one. He passed both notes to Rhodri, who jerked his head back and pulled a strange face when he saw them.

'Well, the sooner we find that boy, the better. I've got to arrange around-the-clock surveillance for Waterloo and that isn't going to be an easy task. Half my surveillance team are on holiday too.'

The note was passed around the desk and was met with the same puzzled expression by everyone.

'Tell you what. If I think of anythin', I'll let you know. Come on, kids, your mum'll be showin' off with her new jetpack if we don't get back soon. Prob'ly trying to do loop-the-loops with it!'

Charlie followed Uncle and the others out of the inspector's office.

So, this is all my fault then, just because I hate maths, and Snitters hates me. Steal some custard, cause her to be attacked, then Allsop's kidnapping, get my uncle's farm shot up with rockets ...

His mind flashed back to the peaceful setting of Drakepuddle Farm. He pictured Auntie turning the small key to stop the chimes sounding on the clock in the bedroom. *You don't want them keeping you awake all night.*

He imagined men shooting rockets at the kitchen window as he slept.

Cause my mum to nearly kill herself with a jetpack, get chased down the river and shot at by a load of terrorists.

Now Allsop gets it, unless the kidnapper receives a secret recipe before ...

He heard the door click shut behind him.

'Uncle, stop!'

'What is it, Charlie?'

'I think I know what Allsop's note means!'

49

'It's something you said,' Charlie explained.

'Something *I* said? About what?' Inspector Yarn replied.

'About keeping a lookout at Waterloo station?'

'I said half of my surveillance team are on holiday. What's that got to do with anything?'

'No, before that. What did say about the *type* of lookout?' asked Charlie.

Uncle watched with one eyebrow raised above his glasses.

'I said we need it twenty-four seven.'

'No, you didn't say that. You said *around-the-clock surveillance*. Can I see those letters again?'

Uncle picked up the first of Allsop's handwritten notes and gave it to Charlie.

Charlie read it to himself. He paused before reading out the last line aloud, '*TIME is the KEY.*'

'What do you mean?' asked Yarn.

'Have you got a piece of paper and a pencil?'

The inspector gave Charlie a blank piece of paper from his desk and the pencil from his jacket pocket. He looked at Uncle. 'Do you know what this is about? I've got to organize this surveillance team ASAP!'

'Give him a chance. He might be onto summat,' Uncle said, removing a black, leather pouch from inside his own jacket. He took something shiny from inside the pouch, which looked like a pocketknife. He flicked it to the side and a long slide rule extended from the end. 'Never know when this might come in handy,' he said, detaching the slide rule and handing it to Charlie.

Charlie took the ruler. A small clamp popped out of the end.

'It might be quicker to use this. Clip it onto the ruler,' Uncle said, passing a shiny, silver pencil to Charlie.

Charlie took the pencil. It seemed to fly out of his hand and attach itself into the clamp, like a pin being pulled by a very strong magnet. As soon as Charlie put the ruler down on the paper, it began drawing lines. Somehow, it seemed to know exactly how long they needed to be.

The inspector watched the pencil like it was some kind of mythical creature that had come to life and was flying around on the piece of paper drawing a neat grid. He looked like he was trying to think of something to say but if he had found any words, they got lost before they reached his mouth, it opened and closed two or three times in total silence.

Charlie copied the message onto the grid.

'Look, each line of his first note is seventeen letters long, and there are seven lines. I've drawn a large grid like a huge noughts and crosses game with one letter in each square.

Inspector Yarn picked up the piece of paper and looked at the grid.

'But what about the last line? *Time is the key?*' he asked.

'I know,' replied Charlie. 'It isn't seventeen letters long. It doesn't fit the pattern. *It can't be part of the message.* I think it's a clue on how to decode the rest of the message.'

'But how?'

'Well, the key to unlocking the code has to have something to do with time. Then you gave me the answer yourself! What do you use to tell the time?'

'A watch? A clock?'

'Yes, around-the-*clock* surveillance. The message is a clock code, like you explained on the bus, Uncle. I think he wanted to make sure we understood what he was trying to tell us. That's why he gave us the clue on the *second note!*' Charlie said.

'There's a message in the *second* note?' the inspector asked.

'I hope you will find me before 12 o'clock on the 1st He isn't talking about the 1st of August.'

Charlie picked up the other piece of paper from the desk and waved it in front of the inspector.

'He's talking about the first note!'

50

'I'm not sure I'm totally with you. What do you mean?' asked Yarn.

'Whereabouts on a clock face is twelve o'clock?' Charlie asked.

'In the middle at the top.'

'Where the letter 's' is in the first line. And he said I hope you will find *me* before 12 o'clock. What comes before 12 o'clock?'

'Eleven o'clock? Half past eleven?'

'Or 10 o'clock ... and *then* 11 o'clock? Look at the grid. If that letter 's' is in the twelve o'clock position, what letters are where 10 o'clock and eleven o'clock would be?'

'*M* and *E: me*. "I hope you will find *me* before twelve o'clock on the 1st." And the circles in the centre of the noughts and crosses grids? What do they mean?'

Uncle answered the question. 'It's a circular code, hidin' in the middle!'

'What? Allsop came up with *that?*' Rhodri asked. 'He can't even win a normal game of noughts and crosses.'

'It must have been the IQ-C_2! Look what happens if you complete the clock code starting at 12 o'clock: the middle letter at the top' Charlie said.

He overwrote each of the letters corresponding to 1

o'clock, 2 o'clock and so on, in bold, then handed the piece of paper to Inspector Yarn.

'See, it looks like this!' Charlie drew a circle with his finger over the letters he had highlighted.

'Signal Hill me. He's at Signal Hill! That's what he's trying to tell us! Come on. We've got to get him.'

Uncle nodded at Charlie and winked. Then he turned to Inspector Yarn. 'Well? What are we waitin' for?'

51

Charlie pulled the crash helmet down over his head and fumbled with the straps. Uncle had lowered the gyrocopter into the police station car park using some pulleys and cables that were in an old suitcase on top of one of the wardrobes.

'Are you sure this is a good idea?' his mum asked, helping him to do up the harness.

'Don't worry, we ain't goin' nowhere near the action. We'll be a mile or two from the house where the police think that boy is. Charlie's insistin' on tryin' to help.'

'But why can't you just let the police deal with it?'

'Well, it is kind of my fault that Allsop's been kidnapped. It should really have been me,' Charlie said.

'Just be careful, and promise me that you'll do everything your uncle tells you,' his father added. 'Oh, and *don't touch anything!*' he added with a glance towards Mrs Crump.

'Okay,' Charlie replied.

'Sure you don't want to change your mind, Charlie?' Rhodri asked. 'I don't mind going instead.'

Uncle tapped a camera on the side of the gyrocopter. 'I've set up a video link. You'll all be able to watch from the bus, so no one's going to miss anythin', and you can make sure we're not gettin' in any trouble.'

Doris was barking and jumping up and down so Auntie lifted her up to give Uncle a lick on the face.

'Sorry, Doris, no room for you today.' He switched on a flashing purple beacon. 'CLEAR PROP!' he shouted.

Charlie watched Doris jump up into Auntie's arms. She yapped excitedly as the engine turned over two or three times, then burst into life, causing the whole machine to shudder briefly.

'Pull your visor down, Charlie.'

Uncle's voice sounded very different through the helmet, like someone holding their nose as they talked.

As he flicked the visor down, everything took on a weird green tint. He could see everything in a strange, grainy light, even though it was a dark night.

'You ready?' Uncle said in his tinny voice, tapping the Tradget screen three or four times.

'Yep!'

There was a short burst of acceleration and a lot of juddering. Within a few seconds, everything was smooth again and Charlie found himself looking down over his shoulder at the bus.

A few hundred feet below, he could see Rhodri and the others waving.

'Wow! This is cool!' he said. 'How long will it take us

to fly to Signal Hill?'

'You mean, how long will it take *you* to fly to Signal Hill,' Uncle replied.

52

'What!' Charlie said. 'I can't fly this. I don't know how'

'I remember you sayin' the same thing about ridin' a bike. It's easy. I'll show you what to do.'

Charlie glanced down at the dashboard. 'I'm enjoying the view, Uncle Pip,' he said. 'Why don't you do the flying and I'll just watch.'

'Don't be daft. I'll show you the basics. Don't worry about none of them gauges. Birds don't need 'em to fly, and nor do we. Put your hand on the control stick. It's connected to mine. Just rest on it lightly and follow what I'm doin'.'

Charlie placed his hand nervously on the control column as the gyrocopter levelled off.

'First thing to learn is that you don't have to move the controls much, especially when we're movin' fast. If I want to go up, I nudge the stick back like this. Flippin' 'eck, Charlie, how tight are you holdin' it?'

'Sorry,' Charlie said, noticing that he had been holding the stick as if he would fall to his death if he let go of it.

'That's better! I can feel what I'm doin' now. See, I pull it back and the nose comes up and we start to climb. Did you feel how much I moved the stick?'

'Not really.' He hadn't felt the stick move at all, but he noticed the nose of the flying machine was now pointing up towards the stars.

'Go on. Have a go, Charlie. Don't forget: you don't need to move it much.'

Charlie eased the stick forward and the gyrocopter pitched down into a gentle dive.

'Relax your grip. You're holdin' it like you're tryin' to squeeze the juice out of a carrot!'

Charlie released his grasp slightly.

'That's it. Now level off and try a couple of turns.'

Charlie heard his mum's voice through the speaker inside his crash helmet. 'What's going on? What are you doing?'

'Nothin' to worry about! I'm just teachin' Charlie to fly. He's taken to it well. Must get it from his mum, eh!'

Within twenty minutes, they were approaching Signal Hill, although to Charlie it seemed to have taken no time at all.

'That's it down there; the hill with the mast on top. Look, it has two access roads — one from the south and one from the east — just like the inspector said.'

'Which one is Hampton House?' Charlie asked, re-membering the name of the empty, boarded-up building that Inspector Yarn had said Allsop was imprisoned within.

'There are the two farms. I bet the rescue team are gettin' ready inside one of them barns. We ain't allowed to go over the top. They won't be able to hear us anyway because I've got the acoustic oppositers switched on, but we'd better do as we've been told. You still okay doin' the flying?'

'You bet!' Charlie said.

'We've got to be on the ground in the next ten minutes, in case they need their helicopters,' Uncle said in his tinny voice. 'Fancy having a go at a landin'?'

'Er, I-I-I'm not sure,' Charlie replied. Flying the gyrocopter around in a big open sky was one thing, but landing it on a field in the dark was something else.

'You'll be fine. Come on, I'll talk you through it. There's a smooth section of the field down there, between those trees. It's a bit misty, but you'll be fine'

'What if we crash?' Charlie asked.

'Don't worry. Just point the nose where I tell you and I'll take care of the rest.' Uncle muttered something to himself that sounded like he was going through some checks. 'Right, bring 'er round to the left a bit … bit more … that's it. Now lower the nose a bit. NOT THAT MUCH!'

Charlie loosened his hand on the control stick and pointed the nose towards the fields where uncle had been pointing.

'Can you see that smooth strip between those trees?'

'Yes. Is it near that old brick building?'

That's it. Keep 'er comin' down, gently, gently. Keep looking straight ahead. OH MY—'

Charlie looked up. Out of the misty darkness he saw a lurking giant, metal structure emerge.

An electricity pylon.

And they were flying directly at it!

53

Charlie pushed the stick hard forwards to dive under the cables.

'NO!' Uncle shouted as the control panel lit up with red lights.

Charlie felt the control stick tremble in his hands.

'Let go! Charlie, LET GO!'

He'd been holding the controls so tightly that he'd lost all feeling in his hand. He immediately released his grip and the gyrocopter banked very steeply to the left and a tremendous force pushed him hard down into his seat as Uncle attempted to avoid the pylon and cables. He felt so dizzy, he thought he was going to pass out. There was a metallic sound too, like blades clanging together in a sword fight. Somewhere above his head, he thought he saw some sparks flashing.

It was a few seconds before anyone spoke.

'Blimey, that was close. You almost ...'

Charlie wondered why Uncle didn't finish the sentence.

The two sat in silence as Uncle brought the flying machine around in a wide turn back towards the landing site, this time much lower. Charlie was aware of some shouting going on in his helmet. Somehow, his mind was blocking it out though. He watched the power lines whizz past above his head. The gyrocopter was safely below them this time.

He'd almost what? Almost crashed? Almost flown them straight into the mast? Almost *killed* them both?

The sound of the wheels brushing through the long grass interrupted his grisly thoughts. The ride was suddenly bumpy again, as if he was being pushed across a ploughed field in a wheelbarrow. The gyrocopter quickly came to a stop.

It was only then that his mother's voice came into focus. She'd been shouting for some time, at least two or three minutes, but somehow he'd totally blocked it out.

'WHAT'S GOING ON?' Charlie could hear her yelling. 'ARE YOU OKAY? ARE YOU OKAY?'

'I were ... er ... just showin' Charlie some of the safety features in Jenny, that's all. Nothin' to be worried about.'

Even though his uncle's voice sounded tinny and strange, Charlie could tell that he was lying.

54

Uncle undid his own harness first. He got out and un-clipped Charlie's seat belt and removed his crash helmet for him.

'Out you get, Charlie,' Uncle whispered. 'Let's put Jenny behind that hut, out of the way. C'mon, you can help me push. This grass is a bit longer than I thought.'

Charlie got out of his seat. His legs were shaking.

The two pushed the small flying machine behind an old brick outbuilding. He felt a little unwell, as if he might be sick at any moment and his head felt like it might split in half too.

Even though he wasn't sure he wanted to know the answer, he had to ask the question. 'Uncle?' he started. 'D-did I just almost get us killed?'

'No Charlie, *I did*. I didn't see them power lines. If anyone lost one of their nine lives just then, it was me. Funny though … well not funny, strange.'

Charlie wondered what was so funny or strange about almost crashing into some power lines. 'What?' he asked.

'Well, power lines should show up on the navigation display. They didn't. Not only that, but we clipped 'em with the rotors and all the instruments kept on workin', a bit like … well, like there were no electricity in the cables!'

'Can they be turned off? Could the police have done it?' Charlie asked.

'They *can* be turned off. The whole network is controlled from …' He paused, 'From a secret location. The police won't have turned 'em off though. That'd just alert the kidnapper. Anyway, if they had, I'd know about it. Come on, let's wait behind that old brick buildin'.'

'But we won't *see* anything from there, will we?' asked Charlie.

'I doubt there'll be much to see. They'll be in and out in a couple of minutes and your friend'll be in the back of a van to the police station before you know it.'

Yeah, and back in school before I know it too, and he

won't be my friend either. Charlie knew Allsop would blame him for causing the whole mess in the first place.

'I can't see anything at all. It's so dark up here. At least with the helmet on I could see something.'

'I've got a better idea, I've got a couple of pairs of Ogglefoggles. They ain't quite up to spec yet, but they're pretty good for seein' at night.'

Charlie watched his uncle lean underneath the front pilot's seat to unclip a pouch. He rummaged around in the dark and pulled something out by the strap.

'What the hell's *that* doing here?' he said.

'What's *what* doing there?'

'It's one of your auntie's handbags! Here, 'old onto it for a minute.'

'No *way* am I holding a lady's handbag,' Charlie protested.

'Bloomin' kids!' Uncle swung the handbag over his shoulder and leant down into the cockpit again.

'Aha, this is what I was lookin' for: two pairs of Ogglefoggles. I almost forgot I had 'em. You can see through almost anything with these. If I can work out a way of stoppin' the circuitry overheatin', they'd be perfect; prob'ly better than the night-vision gear those rescue teams are usin' tonight.'

Charlie took the object which his uncle passed to him.

'Put 'em on then!'

'They feel very loose,' Charlie said.

'Just hold 'em against your face for a second or two and they'll adjust to the shape of your head. They have to fit real tight.'

The strap and the pads around the lenses inflated and

175

the goggles felt like they were pulling themselves onto his face with a strange hissing noise. They became so tight that, for a moment, it felt like they might even suck his eyeballs out of their sockets.

'To switch 'em on or off, blink both eyes together twice. If they start to feel hot you should take 'em off right away. It might take a bit of a pull. They remember the shape of your face for an hour or two, so they're easier to put back on a second time.'

Charlie couldn't wait to try them out. It was a struggle to close his eyes, the goggles were that tight, but he managed to blink twice. Instantly, the world changed from grainy, grey night tones into the crispest, brightest colours he had ever seen. Even though it was a dull night, everything was lit up in the type of vivid, bright light only ever seen on the clearest, sunniest day.

'Wow! It's like the middle of a summer's day! Everything is so ...'

'Clear?'

'Yeah, but the colours are incredibly bright too.'

'Wait till you look up at the sky!'

Without hesitation, Charlie tilted his head back.

He let out a gasp.

'Woah! This is the most *amazing* thing I have ever seen,' he said.

Although it was an overcast and slightly misty night, he was looking straight through the clouds as if they weren't there at all and, even though it was apparently daylight, he could see millions and millions of stars in perfect clarity. And they weren't just clusters of stars, but entire constellations. A multi-coloured masterpiece rather than tiny pinpricks of white light against a plain black background.

'I can't believe anything could look that brilliant. I have never seen so many incredible, incredible colours!'

'Like the night of cloudless climes and starry skies!'

'What?'

'Don't they teach you anythin' at that place? Stay here a minute. I'm goin' to check Jenny's rotor blades ain't damaged. Don't move and keep quiet. If you're enjoyin' the view, you can record it. Top option on the left-hand side,' Uncle said, throwing the handbag at Charlie's feet as he walked off towards the gyrocopter. 'Don't overdo it though. It uses the battery up.'

There was no way anyone else would ever believe these colours, not unless they could see them with their own eyes. Charlie activated the recording mode.

As he sat looking at the stars, he wondered if somewhere, near one of those tiny specks of light, there was a planet with a boy sitting on the side of a hill looking in his direction. It made him feel very insignificant. Did anything he ever did really matter? Would it really make any difference if Allsop was never seen again? Maybe it would be better! He looked down and his glance settled on his auntie's handbag. He remembered it blowing about in front of her whilst they were being chased on the river. She never went anywhere without it, but here it was, abandoned on the grass.

He shuffled backwards behind the small brick building, out of view from his uncle and carefully undid the clasp.

With his Ogglefoggles, the contents were easy to make out: a pair of pliers, something he recognized as a stick of

177

lipstick, a box of matches, a pocketknife, a few spanners, some bolts, a roll of something he had heard his father refer to as 'gaffer tape', a pen, various pieces of metal including some tubing and a box of candles for a birthday cake with the word 'danger' written on the packet. He started to become aware of a very warm sensation on the side of his head. It quickly became uncomfortably hot, like it was burning his skin. It became so unbearable that he had to pull the strap off from behind his head to re-move the goggles.

They wouldn't move!

It was as if they were stuck to his face. However hard he pulled, they just wouldn't budge.

Was he going to survive a near-miss with a mast only to get burnt to death by some goggles? Where was Uncle? He couldn't see him anywhere. He opened his mouth to call out but remembered his instruction to stay quiet. He tried to prise his thumb underneath the goggles and wriggle it around. Eventually, he felt cool air rushing in through a gap as they separated from his face with a slurping sound. He managed to peel them away from his forehead and threw them onto the grass. Surprisingly, they didn't land with a thud as he'd expected but instead, they sounded like they had landed on something hard; something hollow.

He struggled to see anything at all; everything was just grey and blurry again. He looked up to check the sky. It was black and studded with boring tiny white dots.

A few minutes later, he could just about make out the shape of something moving. It was Uncle returning through the dark.

'I told you they get hot after a while, didn't I? They'll be cool enough to put back on in a few minutes. Give us that handbag, will you.'

Charlie passed the handbag. He was just about to explain how he'd rummaged through the contents when Uncle started to tell Charlie what was inside:

'Penknife, lipstick, magazine. Blimey! Some Dyna-Candles! Oh, here's what I was lookin' for: a five-eighths spanner. Back in a minute.'

Uncle threw the bag over his shoulder and walked off in the direction of the parked gyrocopter.

Charlie waited for a few minutes; it was dark and very quiet. He hunted around for his Ogglefoggles. They were cool enough to touch again, so he put them back on his head and inflated the straps. He blinked twice and the night flicked back to life. He could see the rescue team advancing methodically across the field towards Hampton House. They were crawling in pairs and stopping frequently.

To Charlie, the black clothes they were wearing stood out quite clearly against the bright, dewy green grass. He knew that without the Ogglefoggles, they were all but invisible.

55

Jasper Allsop was fast asleep. He'd been having night-mares most nights, dreaming that he would never be re-leased from his damp, noisy, underground prison. It was like the music had driven him mad; he could even hear it in his sleep. Whenever his captor visited during the hours of darkness, the music seemed to be accompanied by flashing lights. In his nightmares, he saw the flashing lights too.

Tonight though, as the muffled music sounded away in the background, he was dreaming that he was back in school. He was a model pupil, sitting attentively in the front row. His hair was combed neatly, slicked back into a tidy parting and every time Mrs Snitterborne asked a question, his hand was the first to shoot up. His uniform was immaculate, right down to the glossy shine on his shoes. He had even dreamt that Mrs Snitterborne had in-vited him to tea with Tristan. Strangely, he had been looking forward to it.

All was calm in Jasper Allsop's world. He could just have easily been tucked up in his own bed at home, whilst his parents sat downstairs watching TV.

He had no idea that nearby two teams of twelve highly trained men were advancing towards Hampton House, wearing balaclava hoods and carrying what they wrongly believed to be the very latest, top-of-the-range equipment.

56

Charlie could see that both rescue teams were now in place. The first team had split in two and had positioned themselves either side of the front door. They were crouching with their weapons ready. The second team had also split up; it looked like half of them would enter through a ground floor window, the other half were gathered either side of the back door.

Uncle had been fiddling with his watch. He'd managed to tune it in to the radio frequency used by the rescue team.

'Not really s'posed to know how this works,' he whispered, tapping the watch. 'The radio signal's meant to be scrambled. Don't tell your mum we were eaves-droppin'.'

Charlie heard a voice, which he assumed was the commander of the rescue operation.

'Status report?' the commander's voice questioned from the watch.

Almost immediately, two responses came back over the small speaker.

'Blue team, go!'

'Green team, go!'

Shortly afterwards, Charlie heard the commander's voice again.

'Engage!'

Through his Ogglefoggles, Charlie saw two men smash open the front door with some kind of battering ram. It took two attempts. As soon as it opened, one of the men threw in a grenade. It exploded a short distance inside the hallway.

'That's called a *flashbang*. And they ain't half loud! They use 'em to confuse anyone inside the buildin',' Uncle said.

Immediately, two men burst into the hallway, the laser beams of their rifle sights standing out clearly against the settling dust of the grenade blast. Charlie followed them inside with his Ogglefoggles. Their moving outlines filled with tones of red and orange. Charlie heard a sudden rush of heavy footsteps over the radio link.

*

Jasper Allsop woke up. He sat up in bed wondering what it was that had disturbed his dream. He thought he'd heard something.

*

The rest of the team spilled in through the front door and Charlie watched as they changed from their black, camouflaged clothing to outlines, filled with the same tones of red and orange as the men already inside.

The other team stormed in through the back door and the ground floor window. Half charged upstairs whilst the others quickly cleared the ground floor.

The Ogglefoggles started to get hot again. He was about to take them off, when he noticed something was wrong.

Something was *very* wrong.

57

It was the jangling of keys.

The familiar sound signalled the arrival of Allsop's captor. It sounded like the man was hurriedly fumbling with the lock.

Allsop heard the keys crash to the floor and the man cursed as he picked them up.

The door burst open and the dreadful man almost fell into the room.

'Time to go! Get up! Quick!'

Jasper Allsop saw that his captor was sweating, even more so than usual.

*

'I can see all of the rescue team inside the house, *all of them*, even the ones down in the cellar,' Charlie said.

'Good ain't they, the Ogglefoggles,' Uncle replied. He turned towards Charlie. The starlit sky reflected in the lenses of his own goggles.

A voice sounded through the speaker on his watch, 'Ground floor, clear.'

'B-b-but, if I can see the rescue team,' Charlie blinked twice and peeled the goggles away from his face. They were starting to get really hot now. 'Why couldn't I see Allsop, or anyone else in the building, before they went in?'

The Ogglefoggles were too hot even to hold. Charlie dropped them to the floor.

'First floor, clear!'

Uncle snapped his head in the direction of Hampton House. 'What the—'

'Basement, clear!'

58

Suddenly it seemed very quiet.

Moments before, Charlie had been able to hear men rushing through the house. Now, there was only the tiniest whisper of wind and the distant call of an owl. He felt like *he* was being watched, it was like the stars and the moon were looking down on him through a thin veil of mist.

The silence was interrupted by a radio transmission.

'Building secure.'

'What about the boy?' the commander questioned.

'Negative, sir. There is no boy. This house is empty.'

Charlie waited for a reaction. It seemed like a very long wait.

'What's your assessment?' the commander asked.

There was another long silence. Without his Ogglefoggles, Charlie noticed that the mist was getting thicker. There was a strange smell in the air too. He recognized it from somewhere. He looked up again. He couldn't see the stars or the moon anymore. He looked towards his uncle. Although he was only a few feet away, he seemed to be disappearing into a cloud of dense fog. Charlie lost sight of his uncle altogether. He bent down to pick up the goggles.

Through the misty darkness, Charlie heard the next radio transmission very clearly.

'We've got the wrong building, sir.'

59

'Uncle?' Charlie called out into the fog.

'Here, Charlie.'

He could only just see the end of his own outstretched hands as he felt his way through the fog, towards where he had heard Uncle's voice.

'What's that strange fog?' Charlie asked. 'And what's that smell?'

'Well, if I didn't know any better, I'd say it was …'

A radio transmission interrupted Uncle.

'We have one hell of a problem, sir!'

'What kind of problem?' the commander asked.

'There's a very dense smoke or fog of some kind preventing us from seeing what's going on. Our night vision and thermal imaging is useless. We can't even find our way out of the house. We're blind as bats down here; sitting ducks!'

'What *is* that weird fog, Uncle?' Charlie asked.

'It smells a bit like … *Confogumist*. But it *can't* be!'

'What? Why not?'

'It was a prototype weapon — Stealth Department — but it barely got off the drawin' board. It was too difficult to produce, it needed so much power. And there's summat else …'

Charlie couldn't see his uncle's face, but recognized the tone in his voice.

'What? What do you mean? What else?'

'There's only two people who knew the formula, and one of them is *me!*'

'What about the other one?' Charlie asked.

'That's why it *can't* be Confogumist, Charlie.' Uncle's voice sounded distant as he finished talking. 'The other one is *dead.*'

60

Charlie put his Ogglefoggles back on. He sensed Uncle was doing the same thing.

'What are you doing, Charlie?'

'I'm putting my Ogglefoggles back on.'

'DON'T!'

'Why not?' Charlie had got used to the superhuman vision. Without it, he felt useless; now he couldn't even see his own feet standing on the long, damp grass.

'Batteries won't last forever,' Uncle said. 'We'll make do with one pair between us. Put your hand on my shoulder and don't let go.'

Charlie felt his uncle start to walk towards the spot where they'd parked the gyrocopter. He took a few steps and stopped.

'*What the —?*'

'What is it? What's wrong?'

'The ruddy ground just moved! Didn't you feel it?'

'No!' Maybe it was because he couldn't see anything but his other senses seemed sharper. As well as the strange smell, he could also hear something.

Was it *music?*

'There it goes again!'

Charlie felt his arm being pulled slowly from right to left. He tightened his grip on his uncle's shoulder.

'Isn't that you moving?'

'I am movin', but I ain't doing it meself!'

Charlie felt Uncle step backwards. 'What is it?' he asked. 'What's wrong?'

'The ground's opened up, that's all!'

'*What?* What do you mean the ground's *opened up?*' He guessed his uncle was describing a scene like some kind of small earthquake. 'And what's that sound? That music?'

'It's like a hatch has opened up in the ground. There's a staircase under the hatch too and I don't know what the music is, but it's comin' from down there.'

'A staircase?' Charlie said. 'What should we do?'

'I don't know. It looks pretty damp and dirty down there, and there might be ...'

'Might be what?'

Charlie felt his uncle flinch and take a step backwards.

'What's wrong?' Charlie asked.

187

There was no reply.

'Uncle! What is it?'

There was still no response. It was like his uncle wasn't there any more, and Charlie was gripping onto the shoulder of a statue.

'Don't make me go there.'

'Go where?' Charlie asked.

'To … *that place*. Don't make me go — please don't.'

He didn't know how it was happening, he hadn't turned the Ogglefoggles on, but Charlie could suddenly see again. And he wasn't standing in the middle of a field in a very dark, foggy night, he was sat in the back of a car, an old car. And he wasn't alone either. Next to him there was another boy, clutching a lunchbox and a school bag, and in the front were two adults.

There was something familiar about the boy. He was a couple of years younger than Charlie but he had very recognizable features. Charlie knew him from somewhere, *but where?*

The boy seemed really excited about something.

'You looking forward to your first day at school, Pip?' the lady who was sat next to the driver asked.

Pip! That's who it was! The boy was Uncle Pip, only much, much younger.

There seemed to be some kind of commotion going on outside the car. There was a lot of shouting and people were running in every direction.

'Minatauri!' the driver called as he jabbed the brakes and the car screeched to a halt. 'Get down Pip!'

What happened next was unclear. There were some masked men. One of them was yelling at the driver of the car. There was a lot of noise and some screaming. A strange popping sound suddenly filled the air. Gun shots. He saw one of the men start to remove his mask. *That face*. He had to shut his eyes.

Was he dreaming?

He opened his eyes again and peered into his new surroundings, shattered glass covered the back seat where he had been sitting, there were thin rays of dusty sunshine piercing through small holes which had been punched out by bullets in the side of the car.

He looked to his side, the other boy wasn't there anymore. He glanced down, he was clutching the lunchbox and the school bag. His eyes started to well up. Through tear-filled eyes his worst fears were confirmed. The people in the front of the car were dead.

He opened the door and ran. He didn't know where he was going, he just had to put some distance between himself and the source of the painful pictures that kept flashing through his head. He ran and ran — it could have been hours, or only a couple of seconds — still carrying his lunchbox and the bag. He looked for a friendly face; someone who could tell him everything was going to be okay. Every face he saw wore the same blank expression.

He heard a man shout. 'You! The boy with the bag. Stop!'

He couldn't stop. He was running down an alleyway and was looking for somewhere to hide. It was a dead end. He looked desperately for a hiding place. A row of large bins; the kind that discarded waste from shops or offices was dumped in. He hid behind them.

This couldn't be happening. This had to be some awful

dream. Then he heard the crack of more gunfire.

The cover from a drain underneath one of the bins was open. He dropped his lunchbox and bag inside and heard them land with a faint splash, then he followed inside.

He didn't know how long he'd hidden inside the drain. He was crying himself to sleep but just as he drifted off, he was disturbed by something; something biting his hand, and something scuttling over his face too.

It went dark again then suddenly it was alright. Someone had found him. He remembered them waking him.

Someone was shaking his shoulder. Or was he shaking someone?

'Uncle, are you alright?'

'Sorry, Charlie, I was miles away.'

'What should we do — about the staircase?'

Charlie thought he could feel his uncle nodding his head.

He *was* nodding, wasn't he? For a second or two, Charlie wondered if the statue he was gripping so tightly might be starting to crumble.

There was a moment of silence, broken by a firm and determined voice.

'Got many of them nine lives left?' it said.

61

Charlie followed his uncle, one careful step at a time.

'Are you okay?' Charlie asked. 'Something weird just

happened, it was like I was seeing some kind of dream, and you were in it.'

'I'm fine. Just a bit worried there might be some rats down 'ere. And that wasn't a dream, it was a—'

He suddenly stopped talking again. Charlie felt something brush over his feet.

'What can you see?' Charlie asked. 'What's down here?'

'There're about two dozen steps and a corridor at the bottom. It sounds like that music's comin' from the other side of a door!'

They stopped before they reached the bottom of the staircase. Uncle seemed to be fidgeting about. 'What are you doing?' Charlie asked.

'Just looking inside your auntie's handbag. She might have some matches in here. Ah, here we go, I'll put 'em in me pock—' Charlie heard his uncle shake a box of matches. 'Flippin' 'eck, there's a *whole box* of Dyna-Candles in here too. They might come in useful!'

Uncle clipped two of the candles to his goggles, one behind each ear, and put the rest of the packet back into the handbag. He took another two or three steps down the staircase, with Charlie still following blindly.

'Jeez, these Ogglefoggles are startin' to get hot. I might have to take 'em off for a—'

'What's happening?' Charlie asked, noticing that the music had suddenly got louder.

'The door at the bottom of the stairs just opened.'

'There's a man ... and a boy, Charlie. No. NO!'

'What?' Charlie asked, clutching his Ogglefoggles.

'YOU!' Charlie heard Uncle shout. 'Duck, Charlie!

Get down!'

Charlie ducked, accidentally nudging his uncle with his knee. The pair tumbled down the last few steps. Charlie landed heavily on his back. Something whistled past his head and there was a sound like a heavy cable whipping through the air a few inches above his face. He pushed his head back hard against the ground and shut his eyes. There was another sound, a loud metal clang and the whipping noise stopped. Almost instantly, it was replaced by a hum somewhere overhead.

When Charlie opened his eyes, he could see again.

62

He was looking up a very tall, narrow, wooden staircase.

He could see the steps rising into the base of some kind of thick cloud. As he watched, Uncle scrambled to his feet. It was a cold, gloomy underground corridor. He turned around and saw a weird-looking man standing in front of him. There was something about the man; something about the way he looked; something quite awful and something quite familiar too.

Charlie wanted to look away, but instead found himself staring at the man's face, trying to work out what it was that looked so wrong about him. He didn't notice Allsop or the strange looking vehicle next to him.

'I don't much care for staring,' the man hissed. 'I find it rather rude.'

'Jasper?' Charlie asked, suddenly recognizing Allsop.

Before Allsop could reply, Uncle spoke.

'You!' he spluttered, looking at the man. 'I thought you were—'

'*Dead?*' interrupted the man. 'Killed by an explosion ten years ago? Don't believe everything you read in the military obituaries. I've actually done very well for myself since my ... *demise.*'

'Diabolus Flack! So you *are* teamed up with the Minatauri!'

'No one calls me that any more. And I'm the *brains* of the Minatauri. God knows they needed some. You don't think they could have worked out what you've got at Drakepuddle by themselves do you?'

The brains of the Minatauri, Charlie thought. Well, he certainly couldn't have been the face. And why was this man so keen to get whatever it was? Surely it couldn't be all about the IQ-C$_2$, could it?

'What do you mean? I ain't got anythin' at Drakepuddle that you could use.'

'Lies! You have the mind-control substance.' The man's face had become red and sweaty as he spat out his words.

'*Mind control substance?* What are you talkin' about? IQ-C$_2$? You can't control people's minds with that! You're off your head.'

'You mean *you* can't control people's minds with it. *I COULD!*'

Charlie noticed that Allsop was looking very confused. He was glancing down at his handcuffed hands and it looked as if he was desperate to say something but couldn't remember what.

'P-p-p-' he muttered.

'And the other prototypes from the Flying Fish Cove experiments, they've got to be somewhere. They're not at the Ministry. I'll get to the truth eventually. Do you think the Minatauri would have thought of looking in some filthy little farm to try and find any of that stuff? *I* gave the orders. They've *always* needed someone like me to give them orders.'

'You won't find any weapons at Drakepuddle. It's a far—'

It was like Uncle had been hit over the back of the head with a thick plank of wood. He had suddenly stopped talking and was staring at the man, and he'd gone very pale, as if someone had pulled a plug and the blood had drained out of his face.

'P-p-p.' Allsop was still struggling to say something.

'Uncle?' Charlie asked.

'What's the matter, Clunckle? You just realized it's pointless? Just give me what I want!'

'*Give them orders,*' Uncle repeated. He wasn't staring at the man any more, but at the floor.

'Don't mess me around.'

'"Give them orders," you said. So you were giving the Minatauri orders before?'

'I've been their brains for a long time. How do you think they got hold of any decent equipment?' He nodded towards the strange vehicle, next to Allsop. 'All the time I was at the Ministry, I was able to pass things on to them. That's why I have my riches — almost everything I want — and you're a pathetic, penniless peasant.'

Pathetic, penniless peasant? Charlie clenched his fists.

'All that time you were at the Ministry you lied to me. You were selling Ministry secrets to the Minatauri. And you ... you gave the order.'

'What order? To break into that stinking, shabby old farm? Chase you down the river in your quaint little toy bus? Why would I do it myself? Why risk letting the world know I'm still alive when I could get *them* to come after you!'

Stinking, shabby old farm! Toy bus! Charlie's fists were clenched so tightly they were shaking.

'You never could see the potential of any of the projects we were working on at the Ministry; always too busy worrying about what damage could be done or what would happen if the weapons got into the wrong hands.'

'Hands like yours! Killer's hands. It never mattered how ghastly or inhumane the creation was, you still wanted to make it, just so you could sell it ... to the Minatauri. But why did you kidnap the boy?'

'P-p-' Allsop looked up when he heard himself being talked about. He had a very miserable expression on his face.

'To get to you. To get the formula ... and to observe him.' The man looked at Allsop and smirked. 'But he's been all but worthless. At first, he was some kind of child genius, then the effects seemed to wear off after a couple of days. Now he's nothing more than a twelve-year-old boy of below average intellect. The only use he's been is that from his height and weight I've been able to compute dosage levels for an adult. Now, give me that formula, then maybe he can go.'

Uncle let out a deep sigh.

'Slight problem, I'm afraid. That batch was a bit of an unplanned experiment. I'd have to recreate it in me workshop. I can't just give you the formula off the top of me head.'

Flack pushed Allsop in front of himself. With his spare hand he reached inside his jacket and removed something which looked like a pistol.

He pointed it at the side of Allsop's arm.

'Perhaps this will jog your memory. I want that formula. *NOW!*'

Charlie noticed Allsop stiffen up.

'Don't hurt him. You can have the blinkin' formula, but I *can't* give it to you now. I DON'T HAVE IT!'

Flack grimaced. He pushed the barrel of the object tight against Allsop's arm. 'Any last words before you forget all about this nasty incident *forever?*'

Charlie could tell there was no way out for Allsop; not even the tiniest flicker of hope. He shuffled, and with one of his handcuffed hands, he started to reach into his pocket. He opened his eyes wide and took a deep breath.

'*PI ... IT'S ONE AND TWELVE TIMES TWO!*' he yelled.

Flack turned to Allsop. His already nasty-looking face contorted into a simmering mixture of confusion and anger. He looked back at Uncle with a strange stare, as if he was blaming him for what was about to happen.

Both Charlie and Uncle opened their mouths simultaneously, but the words came out of Charlie's first.

'*NO-O-O-O-O-O-O!*'

Flack pulled the trigger and the dim light of the stair-well was momentarily lit by a flash.

63

Flack pulled the pistol away from Allsop and flicked a switch on the side. 'I haven't injured him, just wiped his memory with an amnesatron pulse. Next time I use it though, it will be different.'

'You'll never get away with this. There's a Special Forces team waiting to bring you in the second you're outside. And anyway, you won't be able to see where you're goin'.' Uncle said. 'It's pea soup out there.'

'I'm not worried about the Confogumist. My ticket out of here doesn't rely on me being able to see where I'm going.'

'So it *is* Confogumist!'

'It's greatly improved of course. It has a much longer range and I've added a tracking mode. Wherever I go, I'll be shrouded by a two-mile cloud of dense fog. No one is going to be able to find me, even if they *can* follow me! I want that formula delivered to Waterloo station by mid-day.'

Allsop looked like he had just come out of a pitch-black deep freezer and was just starting to thaw out. He was totally motionless and his eyes were blinking.

'Where am I?' he said. 'What am I doing here?' He recognized Charlie. 'What are you doing here, Crump?'

'Don't you know? You've been kidnapped!' Charlie replied.

Allsop stood open-jawed, looking completely lost. It was obvious that he had no idea who the frightening-looking man was who was gripping his arm so tightly.

'Don't ask any more questions,' Flack said to Allsop. 'Get onto the Grid-Hopper.' He waved his pistol towards the rear seat of the strange vehicle. Allsop looked at the gun, then at the Grid-Hopper. He clambered obediently onto the seat, still taking in his strange surroundings.

Flack looked over his shoulder towards a closed door behind him. He pressed a button on the wall and the door slid open.

'You know what you've got to do,' Flack said. He glanced towards Allsop as he got into the front seat of the vehicle. 'And you know the consequences of failing to comply.' He placed one hand on the handlebars and aimed the pistol at Uncle with the other. 'I'll leave you two in the care of my Sentry-droids. They'll *entertain* you for the next hour or two.'

Charlie looked through the open door. He could see the outline of four or five advancing figures. There was something peculiar about the way they were moving, almost as if they were shuffling forwards in time with the music.

Flack turned a key on the handlebars of his vehicle and a huge spark ran down the cable attached to it.

'There's one other thing,' Flack shouted, looking at Charlie. 'Now I know what *you* look like, in case the Hunter needs another hostage! Waterloo station. Midday.' He turned his attention towards the human forms advancing towards the open door. 'Later, my little angels!'

'The Hunter. That's what you're callin' yourself these days, is it?'

Flack twisted the handle bars and his vehicle started to shudder. 'I don't much care for goodbyes,' he said.

Charlie threw himself against the wall as the Grid-Hopper rocketed along the cable, leaving a trail of flying sparks, like an airborne dodgem car or electrified zip wire. Within an instant, it had disappeared into the Confogumist, the sparks lighting up the dark cloud like flash bulbs. The heavy smell of electrical arcing and the loud buzzing noise reminded Charlie of the workshop at Drakepuddle Farm, where Auntie did the welding.

64

Charlie watched the figures advancing towards the bottom of the stairwell. As they got closer, he started to recognize their shapes. They were all women and it looked like someone had spent a lot of time and money on styling their hair. They were dressed in matching black clothing, and the way they were marching towards the stairwell was as if they had gone to tremendous lengths rehearsing their moves. It was all perfectly in time with the music.

They *were* dancing.

Only it was a dance which involved swinging some

very sharp-looking swords. They were a baton-twirling team … of butchers.

'What the 'eck?' Uncle said. 'I'm not sure what that lot are up to but I don't think they're coming to admire your auntie's handbag!'

The Sentry-droids' eyes suddenly lit up in a very intense green, making them stand out markedly against the dim background of the hallway.

Uncle plucked one of the Dyna-Candles from behind his ear and placed it between his teeth. He removed the box of matches from his pocket and lit one.

'Cover your ears and close your eyes, Charlie!' he said.

One of the Sentry-droids raised her arm. The others instantly stopped dancing and twirling their weapons. The leader threw one of her swords. It whistled through the air like a spear between Charlie and his uncle and embedded itself with a thud somewhere behind them. Charlie opened his eyes and looked at his uncle. The tip of the match had been sliced off.

The Sentry-droid's lips formed a narrow smile and she removed something from her belt: a pistol, identical to the one Flack had used on Allsop.

Charlie felt her gaze land on him. It was as if she sensed that he was the lesser threat. Her attention immediately turned towards Uncle and her glance froze.

She jolted her head level and her lips moved. But for a moment, she was silent; it looked like her voice hadn't caught up with her mouth. An instant later, she found the words from her database which best fitted her assessment of the situation.

'Nice *HANDBAG!*' she said, half-shouting the second

part of her sentence. Her voice sounded computerized, but curiously enchanting too.

The other Sentry-droids fixed their glances on the handbag and their jaws fell open in unison.

'Oooh,' one of them said.

'Aaah,' another added, tilting her head to the side.

Uncle lit another match and placed it against the wick of the Dyna-Candle, which he threw to the floor just a few feet in front of the Sentry-droids. It began whistling and fizzing, like a firework inside an old-fashioned boiling kettle. The Sentry-droids were obviously trans-fixed by the screeching, sparkling candle.

Uncle removed another candle from the packet and lit it between his teeth. He placed it back inside the box. As the whistling from the first Dyna-Candle rose to a deaf-ening scream, he threw the rest of the box and Auntie's handbag onto the floor. The Sentry-droids were clearly mesmerized by the strange offering.

'Looks like I was wrong about your auntie's handbag!' Uncle said, picking up the pair of Ogglefoggles that he had dropped on the floor. 'Them lot are lookin' at it like foxes what've just seen a chicken sit itself down on a plate of chips and sprinkle itself with salt 'n' vinegar!'

The noise was almost deafening inside the confines of the passageway as the first Dyna-Candle exploded.

'Let's get out of here!' Charlie shouted, slipping his Ogglefoggles over his head so they hung loosely around his neck.

'Good idea. Hold on tight.'

65

As they reached the trapdoor, Charlie heard several more loud explosions ring out, like a burst of firecrackers, only much, much louder.

A voice cut through the ringing sound, which the exploding Dyna-Candles had left in Charlie's ears. 'I'm seeing lots of flashes and hearing explosions from the south side of the hill. What's going on?' the voice asked from the watch on Uncle's wrist.

'Nothing to do with us, sir!' another voice replied. 'We're hearing it too, but it isn't coming from here.'

'Damn this fog! We can't see anything. We've had power cuts too. If the helicopters can see, then get them airborne. Maybe they can tell us what's going on.'

'Doubt that!' Uncle said.

Charlie wasn't sure if his uncle was talking to himself or not. 'What do you mean?'

'That Confogumist was designed for exactly this purpose. It's got tiny heat particles floatin' round in it so you can't see anythin', even with thermal-imagin' gear. And I think I've worked out how he's got the power to produce it.'

'How? And how's he getting away?' Charlie asked.

'That bolt he fired up the stairwell was aimed at the electricity pylon, the one we almost crashed into. He's using the electricity network to power his vehicle *and* to generate the Confogumist.'

'Have they got any chance of following him?'

'No, Charlie, not a cat in hell's.' Charlie sensed his uncle lunge forwards before he finished his sentence. 'But we might have.'

66

Charlie pulled the straps of his harness as tight as he could and felt the gyrocopter shudder as the engine started.

'Better unplug this! Don't want your folks panickin' now. Here, take it.'

Something thudded into Charlie's lap, and he recognized the shape of the camera that had been attached to the side of the gyrocopter. 'They can get hold of us on your Auntie's radio if they need to.'

Within a few seconds they were airborne.

'I can see their trail of sparks. Sparrow One, airborne from Signal Hill, heading south, following power lines. It's Flack. He's back and he's behind the whole thing. He calls himself the *Hunter*. Sparrow One to Guardian base, do you copy?'

Through his helmet, Charlie heard a crackly voice reply. He thought he recognized it.

'Pip! By the way, *Sparrow*, you've got company. Two helicopters in your nine o'clock at about a thousand feet.

No threat.'

There was something funny about the way the voice said 'Sparrow', as if it was going along with some kind of private joke. Shortly afterwards, Charlie heard another voice. It was one of the helicopter pilots.

'All we can see is a fast-moving fog bank. It keeps changing direction. There are flashes all over the place from inside, but we can't see what's causing it. It's like a thunderstorm rolling across the countryside. We've got no chance of getting down there. We'd have zero visibility, and there are pylons all over the place.'

Pylons all over the place? Charlie's mind rushed back to the close encounter he'd had with the large metal tower earlier. 'How high are we flying?' he asked.

'He's using the power lines to escape,' Charlie heard his uncle explain over the radio. 'High enough, Charlie, don't worry, I can see everythin' through me Ogglefoggles.'

Charlie could tell by the sound of the wind rushing over the windscreen and the screaming of the engine that they must be flying at their top speed.

'That thing's too quick for us, Charlie. We'll never catch it. We used all our rocket fuel on the river. Our only hope is to try and head it off.'

'What do you mean?' Charlie asked.

'If I can see when he's going to turn, I could cut the corner. But those lines run pretty straight.'

Something about his uncle's words repeated in Charlie's mind. *Cut the corner? Cut the—?*

'Couldn't we get them to cut the power? To switch off the electricity?' he asked.

'We could get it switched off, but he'll have thought of that. Prob'ly got some kind of crazy nuclear battery on board as a back-up or summat. Gosh these Ogglefoggles are startin' to get hot.'

'Are you okay?' asked Charlie.

'Flippin' 'eck, he's jumped onto a train line.'

Charlie sensed they had changed direction, and was starting to feel quite dizzy. Without being able to see anything, the buffeting and shaking was starting to make him feel queasy too.

'Sparrow to Guardians. Seems his Grid'opper can use any form of overhead electrics. Guardian One, do you copy? Are you there, George?'

Somewhere deep beneath the village of Great Disbury, a telephone handset was replaced on its cradle with a click. Shortly afterwards, Charlie heard the voice speak calmly through his helmet again.

This time he was *sure* he recognized it.

67

'If *I* may be permitted to make a suggestion, gentlemen.' The voice paused. 'Killing the power in the electricity cables won't stop the vehicle you're chasing. You were right. It *does* have a nuclear battery, Baker has confirmed it. If he uses that to energize the network, there's no telling what damage may be done.'

'So what's your suggestion, George?' Uncle replied.

George? What does he mean, George? Charlie thought. *That's Godfrey Blessings, I know it is! I know it's Godfrey Blessings. And who's Baker?*

'Well, I could slow him down, so you could catch up with him.'

'How?' Uncle asked.

'He must mean slowing them down by controlling the electricity,' Charlie said.

'Exactly! I wondered if he might try to use the electrified railway lines. That's what gave me the idea! I've taken the liberty of connecting one of your controllers from your model railway up to the electricity grid: an old Hammant and Morgan. It might be a bit jerky, but it should do the job.'

'Brilliant! Just like controlling the speed of an A4 class loco on me model railway! Jeez these are gettin' hot again, Charlie. I'm goin' to have to climb out of the Confogumist for a minute.'

Within a few moments, they had emerged into the clear air above the fog bank. Charlie saw his uncle holding his Ogglefoggles away from his face.

'Er, who's flying?' he asked.

'Aah, that's better, a bit of fresh air! Don't worry, Charlie, I've got the stick between me knees. You okay?'

'Er yeah. I could fly for a while if you like. I've got my own Ogglefoggles.' Almost immediately, Charlie wasn't so sure he should have said anything.

'I'll be okay. Just need a minute or two,' Uncle replied. 'Right, George, I think I understand your plan. How long do you need before you can slow him down?'

'Well, it should be working now. I've just finished

soldering the last connections,' the voice replied.

Over the radio, Charlie heard a loud crackling and then a popping.

'Oh blast!' the voice said.

'What was that?'

'I'm afraid I've blown it!' the voice said.

'What! You ain't broke it, have you? The controller? That's a collector's piece that 'un.'

'No, I've blown the blasted fuse. I know there's a spare one around here somewhere.'

Charlie noticed the flashing fog bank change direction. 'Look! He's turned again!'

'It looks like he's heading further north, on the railway line. The voltage on those cables is much less. We might be able to catch him without any help. He's only doin' about seventy miles an hour on that cable. Hang on a minute. There're *two* fogbanks. He's split the Confogumist!'

Charlie looked down, there *were* two large, flashing clouds heading in different directions. 'Which one do we follow?' he asked.

'No way of knowing without the Ogglefoggles, unless you can tell which is the correct trail, George.'

He called him George again! Charlie remembered the words which had been projected on the windscreen of the bus next to Godfrey Blessings, as they had set off from Great Disbury. Maybe George was his real name? Maybe it was a *code name?*

'But what will you do even if you *do* catch him?' Charlie heard the voice ask.

He noticed that Uncle was looking at the map display

on the Tradget.

'The problem might be catchin' him. That railway crosses under another high-voltage overhead power line in a few miles. He'll be off at full pelt again, unless you can find a fuse!'

Uncle lowered the nose of the gyrocopter into a dive and, just as they were about to enter the Confogumist, he spoke to Charlie, 'Just hold the stick dead steady for a moment, will you.'

Charlie placed one hand warily on the rear joystick and held the nose of the flying machine in a steady dive. The wind whistling over the windscreen seemed to get louder as they descended into the fogbank.

'Thanks, Charlie, I've got her now. You can let go. Lucky it's a single-track line. I reckon I can fly out to one side of it and avoid the masts.'

Charlie imagined a forest of pylons and masts with outstretched arms swiping and lashing out at the gyrocopter as it flew through the flashing, foggy night sky. It seemed like there were lots of them. Every few seconds, something whooshed past.

Avoiding them would be a very good idea.

68

As he pictured the pylons grabbing out at him through the thick fog, a thought suddenly formed in Charlie's mind.

'I've got an idea,' he said, 'on how we could rescue

Allsop.'

'Go on. We're gainin' on 'em,' Uncle responded. 'What's your idea?'

'Could we use the arrester hook, you know, underneath the gyrocopter, to hook Allsop off?'

'Brilliant! I couldn't have come up with a better plan than that meself.'

Soon, the gyrocopter was within a few hundred yards of Flack's weird aerial vehicle and still gaining on it. There was a heavy smell of electrical burning in the air as sparks flew off the cable where the Grid-Hopper's contactor brushed along it. Occasionally, something hot landed on Charlie's skin, as if he were standing near a bonfire and smouldering embers were spitting down on him like burning raindrops.

'I'm going to have to keep slightly above the Grid-Hopper, and to one side. It ain't easy. How you getting on with that fuse, George? You're taking your time, ain't you!'

'Your fuses are all over the place. You should be more organised with your storage system,' the voice replied.

Charlie sensed the gyrocopter pitching up and down as it followed the rise and fall of the cable. Maybe it was because of the unsettled feeling he had in his stomach, but somehow, the words just came out … all by themselves:

'Why do you keep calling him George?' he asked.

'Tell you later, Charlie. I need you to drop the arrester hook. We're almost right over 'em. There's a lever by your right knee. Pull it towards you.'

Charlie reached blindly for a lever. 'What does it feel like?' he asked.

'It feels like a lever! There's only one lever on that side. You can't pull anything else!'

Charlie fumbled around. He felt cables and metal bars, and eventually he found something that felt like a lever. He pulled it hard, hoping it wouldn't cause them to crash.

There was a reassuring clunk and the gyrocopter juddered as the hook dropped into place.

'Good, that's it, Charlie. We're just a few feet away now.'

Charlie looked below, hoping he would be able to see at least the outline of the Grid-Hopper. There was nothing.

'Hold your hands out to the right side!' Uncle shouted into the darkness. After a few moments, he shouted out again, this time at the top of his voice:

'JASPER ALLSOP, HOLD YOUR HANDS OUT TO THE RIGHT SIDE!'

Charlie twisted his neck in every direction. He still couldn't see anything.

Then, through the noise of the gyrocopter's screaming engine, the rush of the wind and the sparking sound of the Grid-Hopper, Charlie heard a frightened voice call out faintly from somewhere below.

'Okay,' it said.

69

'He's holdin' his hands above his head but he don't half look confused!' Uncle said.

Charlie imagined being in Allsop's place. What must have been going through his mind, hearing someone calling out his name and shouting instructions from the dark sky above?

'This is hard work, Charlie. They keep wobblin' from side to side, as well as goin' up and down between the masts. Nearly there … *nearly there!*'

Charlie pictured the hook floating above Allsop's outstretched hands. He clutched his Ogglefoggles.

'Just a few more inches,' Uncle said.

Something whipped past above their heads.

Slowly, he lifted the Ogglefoggles towards his face. He pushed them against his forehead with one hand and pulled the strap carefully over his head with the other. They quickly sucked themselves to his face.

Although he was covering the goggles with his hand, he blinked twice. The Ogglefoggles switched on. Charlie wasn't sure what he'd expected to see, but it definitely wasn't the skeleton of his own hand. It was like an X-ray projected on top of a colourful, clear picture. Between the bony fingers, he could see the Grid-Hopper dangling a few feet below. He took his hand away from his eyes.

Allsop's terrified face was staring blankly back at him, holding his handcuffed hands up above his head. The arrester hook was hovering very close to the chain between Allsop's wrists, but every time it seemed to get close, it jolted away again.

As the Grid-Hopper approached a mast, Charlie noticed one of its contactor arms swing around to the front and extend towards the cable on the other side. It sent a shower of sparks high into the air as it let go with the trailing arm. It was like a mechanical monkey swinging effortlessly through a flashing, metal jungle. No wonder Uncle was finding it hard to get the hook near Allsop's outstretched hands.

Charlie glanced up again. There was a small road bridge ahead. His uncle must have seen it at exactly the same moment because he pulled back hard on the control column. The gyrocopter pitched up sharply, forcing Charlie down into his seat. He tried to move his arms up to cover his eyes but he couldn't; they were too heavy, as if his sleeves were made of lead. Several red lights started flashing in the cockpit and a loud bell began chiming. Charlie closed his eyes and waited for the impact. The wheels of the gyrocopter brushed against some moss on top of the wall and there was an awful crashing sound, like a wrecking ball smashing through the side of a house. Something had hit a part of the bridge. It was the arrester hook. It knocked out a handful of bricks but, although the gyrocopter juddered violently, it was still flying.

Charlie's heart beat fast and erratically. The engine coughed and spluttered, missing a few beats of its own. He looked down over his shoulder. The hook was bent slightly, but it was still in one piece.

'Nearly had 'im, Charlie. But a bloomin' bridge got in the way. Hold on, I'm goin' in for another pass.'

'Charlie, can you hear me?' There was a new voice on the radio. It was Bryony.

'Can you hear me? We heard a crash of some kind, but we're totally blind. Is the camera turned on? We can't see.'

'Don't worry 'bout us,' Uncle replied. 'We'll be back on the ground any minute. Just keepin' an eye on Allsop.'

Charlie wasn't so sure that they'd be on the ground as quickly as Uncle claimed. The way the Grid-Hopper was weaving and darting was going to make it very hard to hook Allsop. He watched as they moved into position again. The arrester hook wobbled above the Grid-Hopper and the scenery along the railway line flashed past below. The hook was just behind Allsop now, and inching slowly towards his still-outstretched hands. Allsop's hair was being blown wildly all over the place and Flack's angry face was scanning the sky above, looking for the voice which was shouting instructions at his hostage.

The hook got to within two or three inches of Allsop's hands, Charlie watched as one of the contactor arms swung around to the side and suddenly, Flack's vehicle veered off, following the contactor arm. It accelerated away, leaving a trail of sparks.

Charlie looked up again.

He knew he was as close to death as he had ever been.

70

They were on a collision course with an electricity pylon. And from what Charlie could see, his uncle hadn't noticed.

'LOOK OUT!' he yelled. Instinctively, he blinked twice and everything went dark.

There was no way the gyrocopter could climb. Not without hitting one of the power lines.

He couldn't see anything, but there was a very loud buzz from the power lines and it sounded close ... too close.

For a moment, he imagined he was about to be zapped and frazzled, like a giant wasp landing on an electric fly-killer. Several loud warning chimes sounded immediately.

Charlie felt himself floating. He wasn't sitting on his seat anymore.

His arms and feet were waving around in front of him too. He was ... *weightless*.

Was this what it felt like to be dead?

He hadn't heard a crash though, and apart from something pushing down hard and digging into his shoulders, he hadn't *felt* anything either.

It took a few seconds for Charlie to realize that he was still alive. It was the harness he could feel, keeping him inside the gyrocopter. There was a familiar voice too. It was Bryony again.

'We think you should land,' she said.

'In a minute,' Uncle said.

'But this wasn't planned and, before she fainted, Charlie's mum reckoned that you'd crash any second.'

'We're okay, Bryony,' Charlie shouted, not sure if she would be able to hear him or not. He peeled his goggles off. He'd seen enough close encounters with bridges and pylons.

'Damn! This high-voltage cable means he can outrun us. We'll never catch him, although it does turn in five or six miles, so we might be able to head him off. Any luck with that fuse, George?'

'I think you only had one or two spares with a sufficient rating. I'm sure I saw one in the tin. Delta's gone to have a look, and Papa finally got through on the G-phone to the Prime Minister about a possible nuclear power spike. A few of the Guardians are on it!' the voice replied.

George? Papa? Delta? Prime Minister! What kind of quiz team was this?

The gyrocopter climbed out of the Confogumist.

As soon as they were in clear air, Charlie could see again. There was a glimmer of orange against the pale blue horizon.

'These ain't half gettin' warm!' Uncle said removing his goggles. 'You okay back there?' he asked, briefly turning round to check. The skin around his eyes looked puffy and blistered.

Compared to the buffeting at the low levels and the

noisy trail of sparks they had been chasing, it all seemed calm and tranquil. Charlie watched the flashing cloud racing across the gently rolling hills.

He had a feeling the peace wouldn't last. He was right, a warning light lit up on the instrument panel.

'Now what?' Uncle said. 'Not again!' He tapped the fuel gauge with his finger as if this would replenish the tank.

'This is gonna be tight! We've got five minutes of fuel and we won't catch 'em for three minutes.'

Charlie watched as his uncle placed the Ogglefoggles gingerly over his face, resisting the urge to put his own goggles back on. They were in a steep dive and getting faster as they entered the fog bank once again.

'They seem to be slowing down a bit. Is that you, George?' Uncle asked over the radio.

'We found a four million amp impulse fuse in the tin with your spare watch batteries. You really ought to be a bit more organised with your storage system. How much do you want me to slow him down?' the voice replied.

'If you can get 'em down to about forty knots, that'd be perfect.'

'I'll turn your controller to a setting of about one and a half. Let me know what happens.'

The Grid-Hopper slowed again, this time with a pro-nounced jerk.

'You've overdone it. He's come to a complete stop!'

The gyrocopter whooshed past the stationary, dangling vehicle. The rotors sliced through the air just inches from the cable and passed between two of the outstretched arms of a pylon.

'We've overshot 'em, Charlie. I'll have to go round for another pass!'

'It's the contacts on your controller. They're a bit worn,' the voice said.

'You'd better do summat fast. He's fiddlin' with some switches!'

Charlie imagined the Grid-Hopper dangling back and forth from the cable, having come to a sudden stop. Would Allsop try and jump off?

Charlie's thoughts were interrupted by the sound of Uncle shouting into the radio.

'Get him movin'. I think he's about to energize the nuclear battery!'

A split second later, the Grid-Hopper accelerated.

'Too fast. The boy almost fell of the back seat!'

'I'll try and do it more smoothly this time. You need to put some oil on this controller,' Godfrey Blessings said.

'That's it. Slow 'em down nice and gentle. I don't think he even knows what we're doing. Hold on, Charlie, we're quite close again. If I can snatch him off at the lowest point, we won't need to worry about hittin' a mast.'

Charlie looked below. Without his Ogglefoggles, he was totally blind.

'Twenty feet away at the most. Just keep holdin' your arms still. That's it. Ten feet … five feet … 'Ang on. What's that?'

'What's what? What's wrong?' Charlie asked, lifting the Ogglefoggles back towards his face.

'He's holdin' summat in his hand. It's flappin' around in the wind!'

What could be so important, Charlie wondered, that you wouldn't let go of it when someone was trying to rescue you from a flying motorcycle in mid-air?

He put the Ogglefoggles back on but couldn't bring himself to open his eyes.

'Just a few more inches. That's it. Keep them hands still. No! No! Not now!'

'What? What is it?' Charlie opened his eyes wide. He couldn't see anything. He remembered he had to blink twice. His world burst into brilliantly clear colour again. He looked down. Allsop's outstretched hands were wobbling just below the arrester hook. As Charlie watched, the hook bounced off the chain between the handcuffs and there *was* something in Allsop's clenched fist: a screwed-up piece of paper.

'Not now. Please! Not now! Just a few more sec—'

Charlie snapped his head up. He couldn't see any masts or pylons. 'What is it?' he shouted.

'The batteries in me Ogglefoggles have died!'

71

'No time to explain, Charlie! Put your Ogglefoggles on.'

'But—'

'You ain't got 'em on already, have you? We don't want your batteries dying too!'

'No,' Charlie lied.

Charlie moved his hands up towards his face. 'Can't

you wear them?'

'No! No time. They're set to the shape of *your* face!'

Charlie looked down, he noticed the arrester hook was too low. It was bouncing off a tank of some kind behind Allsop's knee.

'Look at the hook. Is it still close to the boy's hands?'

'It's quite close, but you're too low, and you need to come forward!'

'How much?'

'About the height of a kitchen table,' replied Charlie, 'and forward by about a Doris.'

Uncle made a small correction.

'Too much!' shouted Charlie. 'You're too high now.'

'You're gonna 'ave to do this, Charlie! It's hopeless, I'm flying totally blind.'

Very reluctantly, Charlie placed his hand on the rear control column.

'Whatever you do, don't get the hook caught on any part of that Grid-Hopper. If you do, he could drag us right into one of the pylons.'

Maybe it was all the time he'd spent playing games when he should have been doing his homework but, somehow, it seemed easier than he thought.

Soon the hook was within an inch or two of Allsop's hands again.

'When you've got him, pull back and to the right, Charlie. There's about 400,000 volts in them cables, so whatever you do ... don't get too close!'

Charlie heard the sound of something whoosh past. He glanced up. The rotors had passed between the arms of another pylon, only just missing the mast. The

Ogglefoggles were starting to get hot now and there was something else. Did they just flicker?

The recording mode was still on! What had Uncle said? *Don't overdo it. It uses the battery up.*

He returned his concentration to Allsop's outstretched hands. They were swaying from side to side slightly, which made positioning the hook very difficult. It bounced against Allsop's wrist then landed on top of the handcuffs. It rested there for what seemed like a very long time before eventually slipping backwards. It fell underneath the chain. Charlie pulled back on the stick and felt a slight judder.

The Ogglefoggles flickered again.

'Have you got him?'

Charlie looked down. The hook *had* connected with the chain between Allsop's wrists.

He remembered Uncle's words and pulled back and to the right.

Nothing happened!

'I think it's stuck. Nothing happens when I move the controls!'

'You ain't got the hook attached to the Grid-Hopper, have you? Can you see what it's snagged on?'

'No, it's hooked onto Allsop's chains, but nothing happens if I pull back.'

'It's the extra weight! Pull back harder, and to the right, but watch the cables!'

Charlie looked ahead. He hadn't noticed it before but the brilliant colours were starting to drain from his vision and the display definitely *was* flickering. He could only just see and the next pylon approaching. Ignoring the uncomfortable heat around his eyes, he put his other hand on the control column and pulled back hard, yanking Allsop from his seat. Charlie looked up. The rotor blades were dangerously close to the power lines. He ignored Allsop's screams and pushed the control column hard over to the right and the tip of the rotor blades clipped one of the cables. Sparks flew in all directions and the instruments on the control panel died. The engine started coughing and spluttering. It gasped in its last lungful of fuel and then stopped.

The only noises Charlie could hear were Allsop screaming, the buzzing and sparking of the Grid-Hopper disappearing into the distance, the rotor blades whipping through the air, and the sound of his uncle … whistling.

72

'THE ENGINE'S STOPPED! WHAT DO I DO NOW?' Charlie yelled.

'Just get it level at about waist height above the ground.'

'Won't somebody please tell us what's going on?' Bryony was shouting over the radio.

'Not now, Bryony!' Charlie replied.

'But it sounds like it's all going horribly wrong!'

She was right. And it was getting worse. Everything was becoming dim and grainy. Charlie could hardly see the ground below.

'You're quite slow now. Just let it float onto the grass.'

'Can you see anything?' Charlie asked.

Uncle didn't reply. 'START RUNNING JASPER!' he shouted instead.

Allsop began a weird aerial dance, his dangling legs occasionally stumbling as his feet brushed against some of the longer grass.

Charlie heard a whooshing and looked up. Small jets had fired in the tips of the rotor blades and they began to spin more quickly. Uncle must have done something because Charlie definitely hadn't.

They landed smoothly onto the ground.

'I told you there'd be time for a spot of fishin' later, Charlie,' Uncle said. 'Bet you didn't think you'd catch summat as big and ugly as that though! Sparrow One, we've got the boy. Good pass by Charlie, I knew he could do it. Flack's gone though, George. I think you're going to have to restore full power. We don't want that nuclear battery energizing the grid. It's nearly breakfast time and folk everywhere would be burnin' their toast!'

73

Inspector Yarn paced around the table in the middle of the interview room.

'Can you remember anything at all about your kidnapping,' he asked, 'other than what you've already told us about the escape vehicle?'

'No, nothing!' Allsop replied, sounding very grumpy. 'I don't even remember *being* kidnapped. The first thing I remember is being told to get onto the back of that motorbike thing, then rocketing off into some strange, smelly fog.'

Charlie watched the inspector walk towards the window. He looked tired.

'That ... *motorbike thing* hasn't been found. There were over eighty fog trails in the end. We followed up on all of them as best we could, but found nothing. They all evaporated at exactly the same time.' Yarn turned to Uncle. 'That friend of yours ... he says there's no way of knowing which was the real trail.'

'Correct. If anyone could find him, George could.' Uncle gave Charlie a knowing look that said, *Don't say a word.*

Charlie got the message. *But ask about the note*, he thought. *He must have written it before he lost his memory.*

'How about the ... er ... Sentry-droids? Do you remember anything about them? We found five shiny cylinders, like silver fire extinguishers. We think it's them. One of them has a ripped leather strap coming out of a join in the side, but it's like trying to prize open stones. They're totally sealed shut. There was nothing much else left inside the burnt-out remains of your kidnapper's hideout.'

'No, I only saw them at the bottom of those stairs, dancing with their swords.'

'Oh them machete majorettes! They were a bit scary, eh. That leather strap's prob'ly what's left of Auntie's handbag.'

Why wasn't he asking about the note? It was right there, on the table.

The inspector walked back to the centre of the room. 'Which brings us onto this.' He pointed towards the crumpled piece of paper at last. 'Does it mean *anything* to you? Anything at all? You must have thought it was important, as you were holding onto it so tightly when you were rescued.'

'No. I don't even remember writing it. I already told you!' Allsop replied.

'How about you? Does it mean anything to you?' Inspector Yarn pushed the crumpled note towards Uncle who, without looking at it, passed it straight to Charlie.

Allsop had been avoiding eye contact with Charlie, but now Charlie sensed a vengeful gaze burning into the side of his head as he picked up the note.

He studied the writing. It was the same, neat writing that Charlie recognized from Allsop's other notes. He read it silently to himself:

> *So I am rescued at long last*
> *But did you lousy bozos spot what*
> *I ventured to tell everyone?*
> *It took ever so long*
> *Brainy people are supposed to be quick, aren't*
> *they?*
> *But what is the truth?*

Who did he think he was calling other people *lousy bozos?* And what was he doing *venturing?* Why wasn't he just *trying*. The effects of the IQ-C$_2$ had clearly gone to Allsop's head in more ways than one.

'Make any sense?' Yarn asked.

'No!' It's kind of ... well, *rude,* isn't it?'

'Hmm, it is surprisingly—'

'Surprisingly what?' Allsop interrupted.

'Give it 'ere,' Uncle said, snatching the note and reading it. 'Bloomin' 'eck, What a cheek. The truth eh?' He tapped his fingers on the desk and rubbed his chin. 'I reckon the truth is you need a portion of humble pie to go with that custard. We risked our necks gettin' you freed.'

Allsop didn't say anything. He sat twiddling his fingers and staring blankly at the wall.

It was over two hours later when Charlie and his uncle finally left the police station. As they were escorted out, Inspector Yarn handed Uncle a sealed envelope.

'Take this,' he said quietly, 'but don't tell anyone where you got it.'

Uncle nodded and shook the inspector by the hand.

*

When they were out of sight of the building, Uncle gave the envelope to Charlie.

'Not much use to me. You'd better have this.'

'What is it?' Charlie asked.

'My guess is it's a copy of that note that was on the table. It looked like a load of old gobbledygook to me.'

Charlie took the envelope. 'Can I ask you something?' he asked.

Uncle stopped walking. 'Yes,' he replied, drawing the word out as if to give himself some thinking time. He peered at Charlie over the top of his glasses and wiggled nine fingers around in the air.

'You know your friend? Er, George?'

'Yes.'

'I thought he sounded a lot like Godfrey Blessings.'

'Oh that! Ha! George really *is* Godfrey Blessin's. We all have our own little er ... *nicknames* for each other in the Guardians.'

'You have nicknames for your friends in a *quiz team?*'

'Course we do, Charlie! Don't you have nicknames for each other at school?'

'Not really. What's your nickname?'

'Ha! I'm *Pip!* But don't tell anyone. It's a closely guarded secret!'

'But Pip's your real name.'

'There ain't no rules what say your nickname can't be your real name too. Anyway, it's better than what they used to call me.'

'What was that?'

'Not the Disbury lot, they've always been good to me, but the kids when I was your age used to call me all sorts: dumb, stupid, the loser in the loft, the loft boy—'

'The loft boy? Why did they call you that?'

'I never went to *that place,* not after what happened to my parents. I used to read all day instead ... in the loft mainly; anythin' I could find: books, magazines, newspapers, instruction manuals, anythin' really.'

'What place?' Charlie asked. 'School? But didn't you miss out? School's supposed to be the best days of your life, at least that's what Dad's always telling me.'

'I 'ad loads of fun! I'd take a break to play with me model railway or build a construction kit. I used to like tinkerin' with your mum's doll's house too. Her friends used to come round and take the mickey summat rotten.'

'Didn't that bother you?'

'Nah. They were only jealous about the gadgets I fitted to it. It had almost everythin': solar panels, underfloor heatin', a lift ... even had its own telephone number what rang if you phoned it! I reckon you're the one missin' out. Fancy not havin' a nickname. Tell you what, we'll give you one! You any good at quizzes?'

'I'd never be good enough for your team. Anyway, haven't you got enough people in it already? I heard God — I mean *George* — say he'd spoken to the Prime Minister. Is he in the team too?'

'Ha! That's a good 'un! We're very careful who we let in. You have to be invited, and anyway — you have to pass tests and all sorts.'

'In case they find out what you've got at Drakepuddle? Like Flack said?' Charlie knew he was taking a risk, but Uncle seemed to have opened up. Maybe, for once, he wouldn't mind talking about something delicate.

Uncle nodded. 'I thought you'd ask about that. Flack was hintin' at stuff he knew about from the Flyin' Fish Cove days. I reckon that must be why he tracked me down. It ain't at Drakepuddle though. Not interested in any of that old-fashioned stuff anymore. The truth is ... well, we do have some stuff that could be dangerous in the wrong hands and even some valuable stuff, but nothin' Flack could get hold of. You don't need to worry about that. Your auntie makes sure everythin' is safely locked up.'

'What kind of dangerous and valuable stuff?'

'Oh, you know … a few rifles, couple of tanks… and the most valuable thing's prob'ly your auntie's record collection!'

'A couple of tanks?'

'Only the Guardians are supposed to know about Drakepuddle's secrets, Charlie. Let's keep it like that, eh? Now, no more questions for the time bein', unless it's one about music!'

'But what about that weird daydream I had? Before we went underground? When I was in the car with you.'

'Dreams are funny things, Charlie. We don't choose them — they choose us.'

74

Charlie was woken by his bed shaking him from side to side, slowly at first, then quite violently. The sirens and klaxons were getting louder and louder. As usual, the noise didn't wake him. The sounds barely registered in his sleepy mind.

After the usual twenty-three seconds, the bed slowly started tilting away from the wall. Charlie stirred a little. Then, as the bed reached the critical angle, he was tipped into a slumbering heap onto his bedroom floor. Of course, the duvet and the pillows remained in place.

A dark cloud seemed to be forming inside his mind. He quickly realized why: it was the first day of term.

His school uniform was hanging neatly on a hanger

from a knob on his wardrobe door. His mum had put it there the night before, after he'd gone to bed. Five minutes later, the same uniform was hanging much less neatly from Charlie.

As he twisted the handle of his bedroom door, something fell to the floor. He picked it up and rubbed the metal surface with his thumb and read the inscription.

For Valour

He remembered how Uncle had protested when he'd tried to return the medal. *Why don't you look after it for a while? You've earned it.*

75

When Charlie walked into the school playground later that morning, it seemed to suddenly go very quiet. Everyone seemed to be looking at him strangely too. Some of them were even nudging each other.

The only noise he could hear was the sound of his own footsteps crunching through the gravel. Soon though, a ripple of whispers started to break out from behind him. Very quickly, it became a loud wave washing over the whole playground. He made his way slowly towards Rhodri and Toby.

Allsop stumbled sideways from behind the bike sheds and almost fell into Charlie. Blott and Chugg followed, shoving each other around and pulling at each other's shirts.

'Oi! Watch it lose—' Allsop's mouth seemed to seize shut for a few seconds. 'Oh, it's you. You should ... er ... watch where you're going. You know ... be more careful.'

'I've got some nice cakes in here,' Charlie said, nodding down towards his school bag. 'My auntie made 'em. Nutty fruitcake custard pies. Want one?'

Allsop froze, his mouth and eyes gaping open, staring at Charlie's school bag.

'C-c-custard pies?'

'Tell you what. I'll save one for you. I've got one for Snitters too,' Charlie said.

*

They were still laughing about Allsop whilst they waited to go into the school hall for assembly.

'Did you see his face when you said you had some custard pies?' Rhodri asked.

'Yeah, it was like you'd told him you'd got a man-eating poisonous spider in your bag!' Toby added.

Charlie didn't notice Bryony creeping up from behind. She was holding something in her hand.

'I er ... thought you might want this,' she said. She opened her mouth as though she was going to say something else but she seemed to change her mind. Instead, she handed a small package to Charlie.

'What is it?' he asked.

'Oh, it's a new pencil case. Poppy and me designed it.'

Charlie took the package. Poppy was standing quietly behind Bryony. She looked away when Charlie spotted her. He tore through the paper and unwrapped the package.

'So you don't leave your pencils all over the place,' Bryony explained.

Charlie looked at the pencil case. On the lid it had a very colourful picture of a boy wearing goggles and fly-ing a gyrocopter.

'Wow, it's so colourful,' he said.

'And if it gets lost, you should easily find it.'

'Those colours are so bright, just like they were through the Ogglefoggles. You're right. It *will* be hard to lose.'

'No, silly, I didn't mean that. Your uncle fitted some kind of clever transmitter. He said it's called an *over-ere-emitter*.'

Charlie looked closely at the pencil case.

'It's brilliant.' he said, opening the lid. Inside, there was a folded booklet. It seemed to be a list of multiplication tables and geometry facts. Underneath, there were some neatly sharpened pencils, a Pi-co-peaker and his uncle's old slide rule. One of the pencils looked different from the others. It was a shiny, silver mechanical pencil and was attached to a clip, similar to the one he'd seen on Uncle's glasses. Along the side of the pencil, in fancy writing, it said *Clunckle Eversharp MK1* and there was a tiny green light near the tip.

'This is great. Did my uncle give you all this stuff?' he asked.

'No, we nicked it! What do you think?' Rhodri said.

'What? You had something to do with this too?' Charlie asked.

'Yeah. Who do you think helped come up with the nickname?'

'Nickname?' Charlie looked at Rhodri with a puzzled expression. 'What nickname?'

'Underneath. Your uncle wanted it to just say "Charlie".'

Charlie closed the lid of the pencil case and carefully turned it upside-down. On the underside, in neat, swirly writing it said: *Charlie Crump: Codebreaker.*

76

Later that day, Charlie sat at his desk in his bedroom, trying to concentrate on his Maths homework.

It was hopeless. His mind kept drifting onto other things.

He kept fiddling with his new pencil case. The bright colours reminded him of the superhuman vision the Ogglefoggles had given him. He still had them under his bed. He'd managed to partly recharge the batteries, but there wasn't enough power to use them to look through the wall and see what the Turpins were watching on TV.

There was probably just enough charge to use the re-play mode, and he still hadn't watched the recording of Allsop's rescue.

He placed them over his head and they immediately pulled themselves snuggly into place.

He started to watch the replay.

It was blank.

Blank?

How could it be blank? He'd seen the flashing light blinking in the corner of the goggles whilst Allsop's confused face gawped up through his bony fingers.

He scanned the options and eventually managed to get the rewind function to work. Soon, images of Allsop's clumsy mid-air gallop and open-mouthed dive into a huge cowpat whizzed backwards before his eyes. Moments later he was dangling, shouting and screaming from the arrester hook.

Suddenly, something interrupted him.

'Charlie? You finished your Maths homework?' his dad called from behind the door.

He peeled the Ogglefoggles away from his face.

'Er, just doing it now, Dad.'

'No screens or TV till you've finished!'

'Yes, Dad.' Charlie placed the Ogglefoggles back over his eyes.

The rewind had paused itself. An image of Flack holding the pistol against Allsop's arm was in sharp focus.

He blinked once with his left eye to restart the replay.

'*PI … IT'S ONE AND TWELVE TIMES TWO!*' Allsop shouted.

What? No it's not, it's … Oh, never mind.

As the rescue played out in front of him, Charlie's mind started to wander again. It drifted further and further away. He was back in the gyrocopter, whizzing in and out of the electricity pylons like a champion slalom skier.

Some of Uncle's words repeated in his mind.

Good pass by Charlie

He didn't notice the warm sensation against his

temples.

What on—?

It was as if dozens of relays clattered quickly in his mind and fell perfectly into place.

He ripped the Ogglefoggles away and threw them to the floor, without bothering to turn them off.

He jumped to his feet and grabbed something from behind his diary on the bookshelf. It was the envelope that the inspector had given his uncle. He pulled out the piece of paper from inside, almost ripping it, and let the empty envelope flutter to the floor.

With the images of Allsop still clear in his mind, he studied the note on his desk. He scribbled something down and the light in the pencil turned purple and started flashing.

He was right!

It had been easy too, like his mind was working at double speed and the pencil had written so quickly, almost as if it knew what Charlie wanted it to do. Perhaps one day he *would* be smart enough to join his uncle's team after all. He remembered something else Uncle had said. *You have to pass tests and all sorts.*

His thoughts started drifting off again. He imagined himself sat around a large table, eating crisps and answering difficult questions about Art, History, maybe even Maths. Something caught his eye;- something glistening in the last rays of the setting sun. It was the medal, hanging from the doorknob.

Good pass by, Charlie.

And then he started wondering …

how many tests?

Great Disbury Guardians - Fact File

TOP SECRET

The residents of Great Disbury had one of their long
meetings and decided it would be safe to share some of
this secret information with you. Some of the Guardians
were a little unsure at first but they were eventually
persuaded. Many of them are not at all keen on blowing
their own trumpets, so they asked if they could keep one
or two things secret for the time being, and they hope
you'll understand why. It would have been nice for them
to have given a *little* more away, but anyhow, this is how
they wanted it.

They are *The Great Disbury Guardians* and are listed in
alphabetical order:

Codename: Baker
Real name: Betsy Byron
Specialisms: Poetry, Baking
Address: The Old Bakery, High St, Great Disbury

Codename: Bravo
Real name: Classified (Guardian under training)
Specialisms: Classified
Address: (Not yet resident)

Codename: Candle
Real name: Classified (Guardian Grand Principal)
Specialisms: Classified
Address: Classified

Codename: Charlie
Real name: Classified (Guardian under training)
Specialisms: Codebreaking, Curiosity, Cycling
Address: (Not yet resident)

Codename: Delta
Real name: Dorian Dobson
Specialisms: Art, Sculpture, Table Tennis, Caravanning
Address: Lott's Cottage, The Green, Great Disbury

Codename: Freddie
Real name: Quentin Tobias (QT) Fitchett
Specialisms: Materials Science, Production Engineer-
              ing, Cartography, Geocaching
Address: The Olde Forge, Station Lane, Great
              Disbury

Codename: George
Real name: Godfrey Blessings
Specialisms: Mechanical Engineering, Fluid Dynamics,
              Motor Racing
Address: The Post Office, P1 High Street, Great
              Disbury

Codename: Mike
Real name: Mihangel Merryweather
Specialisms: Classified
Address: Keeper's Gate, School Lane, Great
Disbury

Codename: Papa
Real name: Buster Planck
Specialisms: Theoretical Physics, Quantum Theory,
Punk Rock Music
Address: Chaos Cottage, Durdle Drive, Great
Disbury

Codename: Pip
Real name: Peregrine Clunckle
Specialisms: Military Inventions (& other Apparatus),
Military History
Address: Drakepuddle Farm, Great Disbury

Codename: Tango
Real name: Tilly Turing
Specialisms: Mathematics, Martial Arts, Jam,
Marmalade and other Preserves
Address: -1 Origin Alley, Great Disbury

Codename: Victor
Real name: Victor (Vic) Twenny
Specialisms: Computing, Meteorology, The Potato
Industry
Address: The Chip Shop, 20 High Street, Great
Disbury

Charlie Crump – Codebreaker!

Allsop's coded message

l	a	m	o	k	T	h	i	s	m	a	n	h	a	s	n	t
h	u	r	t	m	e	y	e	t	I	m	i	s	s	a	l	l
o	f	m	y	f	a	m	i	l	y	G	i	v	e	t	h	e
f	o	r	m	u	l	a	a	n	d	a	n	y	o	n	e	s
w	o	r	r	y	s	l	i	p	s	a	w	a	y	b	u	t
a	s	h	e	i	s	w	i	l	l	i	n	g	t	o	g	o
a	n	y	l	e	n	g	t	h	t	o	f	i	n	d	i	t

TIME is the KEY

Each of the letters corresponds to the position of a
number on a clock face.

The "s" is in where the "12" would be. The "l" is where
the "1" would be and so on. The "m" and the "e" are at
the 10 o'clock and 11 o'clock positions.

'I hope you will find me before 12 o' clock on the 1st.'

Charlie Crump – Codebreaker!

ABOUT THE AUTHOR

Jack Swift was born in Staffordshire and moved all around the country, eventually settling somewhere near the middle of it, and not that far at all away from where he started.

Having been useless at Maths, English and most other subjects at school, he was told to ignore his boyhood dreams and get a job which suited his limited abilities. He tried various things to earn a living including cleaning out chicken sheds, working on a cheese counter, driving delivery vans and making the inside of toilet rolls.

Eventually he stopped listening to the good career advice. He now flies jets and writes books. He lives with his wife and children, quite close to the home of the Codebreakers.

73326069R00149

Made in the USA
Columbia, SC
10 July 2017